❧ Contents ❧

For Marion, Lewis and Harriet

Chapter 1 ✤ A Curse

THE SCHOOL WHERE I FIRST MET CORA RAVENWING WAS called Okington School, and I was just beginning to have real ideas and opinions of my own when I first went there. There were seventeen of us in the class—all girls.

I was the oldest of three children. My name was Rebecca Stokes; some people called me Becky, some Stokie, and the teachers always stuck to Rebecca in full. My brother Joseph was six when I started at Okington, and little Dorian was two. My father was a businessman, in textiles, and my mother, who had been a teacher, was now at home all the time looking after us.

It didn't take me long to feel settled at Okington, though I hadn't wanted to move schools. We'd moved house because of my father's work and I just had to move schools too. My best friends at Okington were Hermione Phillips, Barbara Foster and Susan Spenser. We had our desks in a block near the front of the class and usually we worked quite hard at the lessons and didn't get into much trouble.

Hermione and I were clever at English, Barbara was best at Maths and Susan was very artistic. She always felt stupid at school but, actually, after we all grew up, she was the only one to make much of a career; she became a dress-designer and I'm always seeing her name in the papers, though we're not friendly any more. In fact, I'm not friendly with any of them any more, which sometimes seems regrettable but isn't surprising in the light of events all those years ago.

Hermione and I used to walk to school together. Our homes, in the little Buckinghamshire village of Okefield, were fairly near each other and I usually met her coming down her drive as I passed. I was quite plump, with short, black hair and a pink face which people used to say looked very healthy. Hermione was rather thin and nervous-looking, with blonde, curly hair cut very short. I was envious of her appearance because I thought she was much more sensitive-looking than I was. The only bad thing about her was that she bit her nails and was always having to bend her fingers round awkwardly so people wouldn't see the chewed ends. So I could at least console myself that my hands were nicer than hers. We used to write a lot of poetry together but, though she never said anything herself, I always felt that I was just pretending while she was the real poetess. She used to screw her face up and say such thoughtful things, while I just systematically plodded through the alphabet, trying to think of rhyming words. Once we had our poems in the school magazine, and I was sure that people were thinking that, really, Hermione, so beautiful and so intense, was responsible for it all and had helped me with mine because we were friends.

Once, instead of going to school, we bought bars of choco-late and apples and went off to the common. It was a beauti-ful spring day and the idea shot into my head out of the blue. I just said: "Let's not go today! Let's keep on walking!"

"Not go!" said Hermione. "Don't be silly. Miss Dingwall would be terribly cross and our parents would find out ..."

"We could say we'd been sick. Lots of people are being sick; there's something going round. Mary Jacobs was sick yesterday and I felt queasy myself. I told Miss Dingwall I did, so she'd be bound to believe me. And I'm always with you, so you'd be likely to catch it too." Hermione still looked scared and started biting a nail. "Oh, come on! Don't be spineless. We never do anything unusual. We need experiences for our poetry, anyway. How're we ever going to write anything interesting if we never do anything interesting?"

That argument seemed to carry some weight. "All right," Hermione said. "We'll go. But what about lunch? We can't just wander off with no plan in mind at all."

"I don't see why not," I said. "Why not just wander off and see what happens?"

"No, I can't do that," said Hermione. "It's too disorganized."

I thought she might change her mind altogether, so I just said: "All right, you organize us. I don't care what we do as long as we miss school and stay outside all day."

Hermione decided we'd have to go to the common; that was the nearest bit of real countryside. She began to get into the spirit of the thing. "It's wide and free," she said. "We can observe the flowers, listen to bird-song, ramble through nature, become a part of it."

"Let's get chocolate from Copcutt's," I said. Copcutt's was the village shop. Hermione wanted something more natural and health-giving; she bought apples and a piece of cheese. We put our supplies in our satchels along with our ties and hats, and we unbuttoned the necks of our blouses and struck out for the common, full of exhilaration at our daring.

We had to pass St. Matthew's Church on the way and, as we approached, a little stick-like figure appeared, running unevenly down the road, her satchel bumping her knees at every step.

"It's Cora Ravenwing!" hissed Hermione. "Now what do we do?"

"Just keep walking," I said. "We never usually speak to her anyway. She won't dare ask where we're going."

The figure stopped running and proceeded towards us at walking pace.

"She's seen us," said Hermione. "We'll have to go back. She's bound to tell everyone she's seen us here."

"No. Keep walking," I said. "Ignore her. I'm not going to let Cora Ravenwing ruin everything—her of all people!"

Hermione didn't really know what to do, but I just plodded on firmly, looking straight ahead, and she followed me. I didn't look at Cora as she passed us, but I think she had a good stare at us. I sensed her beady eyes and jerking little head, with the flapping, black fringe, turned in our direction. After we'd gone on a few yards we heard her running feet again and glanced quickly round. She was pattering off down the road, arms and legs going in all directions, blazer flying open.

"There," I said. "Told you she wouldn't speak."

"I bet she'll say plenty at school," said Hermione. "I must say that's cast a blight on things."

"Oh, rubbish! I'm not letting her wreck the day. And I don't think she'll say a word to anyone. After all, nobody ever wants to hear what she's got to say anyway."

After that we really did have a marvellous day. The sun

brought the best warm smells out of the grass and gorse, and small, bright birds darted in and out of the bushes, and larks sang overhead. We found clear water to paddle in and ate our lunch in a sunny hollow where the grass was silky and smooth. We went home at half-past three, as we would have done from school, and Hermione's mother asked me in for tea at their house as my mother was still there having called in earlier. The two mothers sat in the garden on deck-chairs after Mrs. Phillips had made scrambled eggs and stewed apple for Hermione and me to eat at the kitchen table.

"I think the day's been a total success, don't you?" I said when Mrs. Phillips went outside to rejoin my mother.

"Not bad," said Hermione. "Just as long as that ghastly Ravenwing girl hasn't spilt the beans."

"I'm not going to give it a thought," I said. "We'll just tell Miss Dingwall that we weren't well and that'll be that."

"What about sick-notes?" said Hermione. We were supposed to take notes from our parents if we stayed away from school.

"One day's not going to matter," I said. "We can say we've forgotten them, anyway." I wasn't at all worried.

But all hell broke out at school the next day. Miss Dingwall called us up to her desk as soon as we arrived in the class-room. She asked for our sick-notes, and when we muttered excuses she said she didn't believe us, and then Hermione started crying and confessed the whole thing with no attempt at a cover-up. I hadn't been for lying exactly, but a certain amount of evasion might not have come amiss. Miss Dingwall looked all pinched and stuffy and sent us to the headmistress, Miss Todd, who said some really unpleasant things about dishonesty and idleness which I thought we hadn't deserved. I felt like crying with rage.

Hermione wept non-stop all the time Miss Todd was talking to us and, thereafter, on and off all day. She was heart-broken that we should be in such disgrace with the teachers. Barbara and Susan had to be told the story then, and felt hurt that we hadn't confided in them beforehand, far less included them in the day's truancy. I think they eventually believed me when I insisted that the idea had come to me and been acted upon entirely spontaneously.

I kept looking across at Cora Ravenwing all day and meet-ing those black, beady eyes of hers. Had she really told Miss Dingwall she'd seen us heading for the common? Barbara and Susan said they hadn't heard her say a word, but it was just possible that she had darted up to Miss Dingwall unobserved and said just enough to cast doubt and suspicion in her mind. Hermione was sure that that was what must have happened.

In the art class during the afternoon Susan made a little figure with odd bits of clay that were left over from our coil pots and she sneaked it out of the art room in her satchel. She became very mysterious about it and said we'd see what it was for after school. We left school together, the four of us, and wandered towards the village centre, waiting for Susan to explain herself. She eventually hopped over a gate into a field. "Come on," she said. "This is a good place. Nobody'll see us here." Her smooth little freckled face was quite hard and mean-looking as she pulled the soft clay figure out of her satchel and straightened out its limbs. She laid it on the grass and we gathered round and looked down at it. "That is Cora Ravenwing," she said and glanced at each of us in turn with bright, excited eyes, "and she is *bad*. Do you all agree?"

The others said definitely that they did agree and I said I thought it was possible. "Right," said Susan, "then I'll show you what we do to bad people." She ran over to the hedge, which was thick with brambles and thorns, and stripped off a handful of prickles and spikes of one sort and another. Then she ran back and, with her teeth bared and her eyes staring straight out of her head, she began to stick them into the figure, saying: "This is for you, Cora Ravenwing, and so is this and this and this . . ."

I was taken aback at the spectacle, but Hermione caught fire in seconds. "Wait for me! Wait! Wait!" she cried and tore thorns by the handful from the hedge herself, impervious to the scratches she received in the process. Then she was down on her knees beside Susan, plunging them into the figure. After a while, with no obvious enthusiasm but almost for the sake of form, Barbara followed suit and I was left standing there by myself.

"Come on, Becky! Hurry up! There's hardly any more room," called Hermione, looking up at me, her cheeks all flushed and her eyes still red from the day's weeping. She held out some thorns for me to stick in too—and I did.

When the little figure was packed tight with thorns and looked more like a rolled-up hedgehog than anything else, Susan called a halt. She picked the thing up and held it aloft. "Cora Ravenwing," she screamed shrilly, "we cast you from our midst for ever!" Then she hurled the prickly figure into the middle of a nearby thicket. "There, that should settle her for a bit," she said to the rest of us. "That'll teach her to make trouble for any of us."

"Oh, Susan, thank you," said Hermione fervently. "That was just what was needed. I feel ever so much better now —as if justice has been done, somehow."

"Well, I hope it was justice," I said grumpily. I wished I'd had the strength of mind not to add my share of thorns. "We don't know for a fact that Cora did tell Miss Dingwall."

Barbara spoke then. She hadn't had much to say on the topic hitherto. "I think it's only logical to assume that she did. How else could Miss Dingwall have known?"

"I don't think she *did* know till Hermione broke down and told her," I said. "She was just suspicious of our having no sick-notes. But Hermione felt so guilty she started crying and confessing straight away."

Hermione started sobbing again at this point.

"Look what you've done," said Susan crossly. "She was just feeling better after the most miserable day, and now you've got to start blaming her for the whole thing. Of course it was Cora. Miss Dingwall landed on you as soon as you came in this morning—she jolly well knew that you'd been doing something naughty."

"I don't know," I said. "Let's go home, anyway, and get the rest of it over with. I've still got my parents to tell. I might as well get my excuses in before Miss Todd gets in touch with them."

"Oh, Heavens!" wept Hermione. "What on earth will Mummy and Daddy say? I've never been in trouble before."

"I expect they'll say it's *my* influence," I said testily. I knew the Phillipses weren't entirely enthusiastic about my friendship with Hermione despite displays of great friendliness and hospitality to my whole family. I thought it was because we were newcomers to the village and hadn't proved our worth yet, our house wasn't very grand, and my accent had a distinct Birmingham twang to it. I always came away from their house feeling that I hadn't quite come up to scratch. I picked my satchel up and stumped off towards the gate, leaving Susan in charge of mopping up Hermione.

As I went on down the road Barbara caught me up.

"Listen," she said. "Don't take it all so personally. Nobody's blaming you."

"I didn't think they were," I retorted. "I thought we were all blaming Cora."

"Well, that's probably the right thing to do," said Barbara. "She's a bad lot. She always has been. We keep telling you that."

"I don't understand . . ."

"No, it's difficult if you haven't always lived here, but remember we've known her for years. Our mothers knew her mother. It's just something we all know about—she was born bad."

"That's crazy," I said. "I've heard some of the stories, but it's just malicious gossip; it doesn't amount to anything. My parents think that really too."

"They don't want you to be friends with Cora, though, do they?" persisted Barbara. She was clever at beating one down in an argument.

"No, they don't," I admitted. "But that's only because they like an easy life. They think there's no point our coming here and flying straight in the face of local tradition and opinion."

"There you are, then," said Barbara, as if something had been proved. "Look, don't take all that emotional business in the field so seriously. It didn't mean a thing. We stuck some thorns into a lump of clay—so what?"

"Didn't you see their expressions, though?" I said, looking into Barbara's untroubled, cheery face. "They looked half-demented with it all."

"Just a bit carried away. What does it matter? They'll forget the whole thing by tomorrow. You're the worried one. They've got all their hatred out of their systems now. You're the one who's haunted by it all."

That was Barbara's great strength, that balanced, unflappable clearsightedness. Sometimes it made her rather unexciting company; one longed for a bit of imaginative flair. But at times like this she could be so nice and comforting. Her matter-of-fact approach began to dull my vivid vision of the feverish, mad faces of the others, and I felt less horrified and repelled.

"You're right, Barbara," I said. "Thanks for coming after me and explaining. It *is* sometimes difficult for me—I haven't been here long and, although I've tried to go along with it, I still haven't really got the full-blown Cora Ravenwing complex that everyone else has grown up with. Perhaps it'll develop." I asked her to tell Hermione and Susan that I was sorry for being horrid and that I'd be all right tomorrow. She said she would and then she turned back to where she'd left them and I went home.

I told my mother about the truancy that evening and she was shocked at first, but seemed not to mind so much when she realized that I liked school really and wasn't intending to repeat the incident. When my father came home she told him too but represented the escapade almost as evidence of my developing independence and imagination. So he was very jovial and just whacked me on the behind and said: "On no account do this again, understand? And toe the line for a few weeks till it's all well and truly forgotten."

I didn't tell either of them about Susan's clay figure and what we had done to it, but that night I had dreadful dreams and later woke and was very sick. Mother remarked that it was judgement from Heaven and kept me at home for a day. She was very careful to provide the statutory sick-note for Miss Dingwall on my return to school.

Chapter 2 ❧ Cora

WHEN WE FIRST ARRIVED IN OKEFIELD IT WAS THE BEGINNING of the summer holidays. Father's new job was in London, so we had to leave Birmingham, where I'd lived all my life, and find a new home near enough work for him to travel to and fro daily. Eventually my parents found the little house in Okefield which we all settled into very happily. The arrangement was that Father should go up to London by train every day. The only trouble was that, as he left early and returned late, we didn't see much of him on weekdays.

I remember the day we all jumped out of the car and first saw the new house. The sun was shining, flowers were out and there was a big white lilac bush outside the front door perfuming the whole garden. Our furniture had arrived by van the day before but had just been dumped in any convenient space, so there was a tremendous amount of unpacking and sorting out to do. Mother and Father were rather appalled at the size of the task and ordered me into the garden with Joseph and Dorian. They said there was just no chance of getting straightened out with the three of us underfoot. We were more than happy to stay outside, exploring our new territory. It was a big garden with a lot of shrubbery where we could hide or make dens. There was a rickety shed too, with not much inside except for old, chipped flower-pots and a length of perished garden hose. A privet hedge, thin in places, ran right round the garden, giving protection from neighbouring gardens and also from the street, which went straight past the house at the front.

The house itself was about a hundred years old, russet brick with sash windows. It had four small bedrooms and a tiny bathroom upstairs and enough space downstairs for us to feel we weren't cramped. It was better than the Birmingham house, where Joseph and Dorian had had to share a bedroom, and Mother was very cheerful about her new kitchen and said that preparing meals might even become enjoyable now she had enough space to do it in comfort.

As we poked around the garden that first afternoon, with Mother and Father shouting and clattering indoors, I began to feel slightly uneasy. I didn't tell Joseph because I thought it was just the fact that everything was strange, but I kept feeling rather as one feels when turning over a big stone— a bit jumpy, ready for something to dart out from underneath, something wriggly or wiry or spidery. In the shed I felt particularly apprehensive—as if the door might slam shut on me or some creature jump out from the shadows. In the open it wasn't quite as bad; one couldn't feel frightened in the sunshine with the flowers so bright and the birds singing so loudly. The boys found a ball in the bushes and started kicking it around on the grass. Dorian stumbled around chuckling, rolling over, and lying flat on his back to point up at trees. He was a sweet, plump, roly-poly toddler and we all adored him. I lay down beside him and tickled him and rolled him over and over till he got hiccups. Then we sat up and looked about for Joseph, who'd kicked the ball right down to the far end of the garden and gone after it. I pulled Dorian to his feet and he bobbed along beside me down the garden path. "Joji, Joji," he shouted and trotted ahead. "Ball pees, ball pees." The path petered out in a jumble of thick bushes and undergrowth, so I picked Dorian up and was about to make my way through it when Joseph's head popped out from behind a spiky evergreen shrub.

"There's a girl here!" he said indignantly. "She's hiding in our garden, spying on us."

"Tell her to come out," I said.

"She won't come. She won't speak. She's just standing here."

I craned forward as far as I could but I couldn't see her. I put Dorian down but he started to scream and stretch his arms out for me to lift him again. "Oh, make her come out, Jo," I said. "Dory's being a pest and I don't want to carry him through all these bushes." Joseph disappeared again and I could hear him telling the girl she'd have to shift, but he didn't have any success.

"I can't make her move," he shouted.

"For goodness' sake come out here and play with Dory," I said. "I'll handle her."

He came jumping out through the straggling mass of shrubs and creepers, his ball under his arm, and soon he'd tempted Dory off down the garden again towards the house. I pushed my way through the twigs and branches till I got round behind Jo's bush and there, sure enough, was the girl. She was as thin as a rake, with a pointed little white face, piercing black eyes and a lot of very straight shiny black hair. She was wearing navy shorts and tee-shirt, no socks, and a pair of sandals.

"What are you doing in our garden?" I asked. She said nothing, just blinked once or twice and dropped her head on one side, staring at me like a bird. "You shouldn't be here," I said. "This is private property. You're trespassing. It's against the law." Still she didn't speak. "I could get the police."

"Don't do that," she said urgently. "*Please* don't do that. I didn't mean to be bad. I thought the house was empty. I was only looking . . ."

"Course I won't," I said, magnanimous now I'd got my way and coaxed speech out of her. "I was only teasing. But we live here now, so you can't just come in when you want any more."

"I shan't," said the girl, pushing her black fringe back from her eyes. "I shan't come again unless I'm asked."

"What's your name?" I asked.

"Cora Ravenwing. What's yours?"

"Becky Stokes. How old are you? You look about the same age as me." I was surprised when we established that she was, in fact, a little older—she was so small and under-nourished-looking. But then I knew I was a bit fat. I hated that. It emerged that she'd had her birthday the previous week. "Did you have a party?"

"No."

"Oh, that's a shame. My birthday's very soon but I probably won't have a party this year either. I don't know anyone here to ask—What school are you at?"

"Okington."

"That's where I'm going! I bet we'll be in the same

class!" I was very pleased to have met a schoolmate already; I'd been dreading facing a class of strangers.

After that, Cora and I talked for a long time. We came out from the bushes and sat on the grass in the sun. I thought she was strange, the way she said so little and sat so still, just staring at me. Sometimes she'd dart a furtive glance across at Dory and Jo, or suddenly shake her hair out of her eyes—odd, jerky movements. But I was glad of her company and glad of an audience. I told her all about myself and my family, and she seemed pleased just to listen. She didn't go away, at any rate.

In the end it was Mother who interrupted. She came to the back door and called me in for something to eat. It was the middle of the afternoon, but I hadn't noticed my hunger because of the excitement of the new house and meeting Cora. "Come and see Mummy," I said, but Cora hung back. I pulled her up and led her by the hand up the path.

"Mummy, this is Cora Ravenwing. She's at Okington School and she's my age, so we'll probably be in the same class, won't we?"

"Yes, I should think you will. Hello, Cora," said Mother.

Cora hung her head a bit and squinted up at Mother. The sun was in her eyes. "Hello," she said and shifted about jerkily from one foot to the other.

"I'm afraid Becky and the boys will have to come in for lunch now," said Mother. "We're all at sixes and sevens today, but I expect we'll soon get organized. Perhaps you'll come and see Becky again another day."

"That would be nice," I said as Cora turned to go. "I could meet some of your school friends, maybe, and then I wouldn't feel so strange at the beginning of term." Cora just waved and ran off.

Lunch was sausages and baked beans and I felt ravenous

as soon as I saw it. None of us spoke much during the meal but I did say how pleased I was to have met Cora and what a stroke of luck it was that she was my age. Mother said: "Funny little scrap. Doesn't she have a home to go to? When's she having *her* lunch?" Then I realized I hadn't asked Cora where she lived, so I couldn't get in touch with her. I'd just have to wait till she came back to me.

I didn't have to wait long. The next day was drizzly and cold. Nothing seemed as good as it had the day before. The rooms suddenly smelled musty and there didn't seem to be enough light. None of us had slept very well in the midst of makeshift arrangements. At breakfast, Mother and Father argued and wrangled over who was to have which bedroom, and Jo and Dory began to irritate each other too. In the end Mother asked me if I'd organize games for the boys in the front room downstairs while she and Father went upstairs to straighten out once and for all. A big, middle-aged woman called Mrs. Briggs, who'd been the daily help of the previous residents, turned up and said this was her usual day for coming and did Mother want to keep her on. Mother and Father both looked very relieved and said it was a marvellous piece of luck and she was just what was needed. Mrs. Briggs looked pleased and was soon capably clanking round with buckets and brooms. I could hear her voice upstairs advising Mother on where to store blankets and cases and which doctor to register with and which dairy to get milk from and which newsagent . . . Her local knowledge seemed endless. I thought she sounded bossy and domineering and I was surprised how grateful Mother seemed. Even Father appeared to find her presence reassuring and began whistling instead of cursing as he hauled bedsteads and mattresses around.

Downstairs in the front room I managed to locate the

box containing the boys' train-set, and they became engrossed in laying out the track and building bridges, stations, signal boxes and all the rest of it. Then I was the only one with nothing much to do, so I sat down by the window with a book. But I felt too disorientated by our move and the chaos around me to concentrate, so I took to staring vacantly out of the window. I could see people walking along the pavement on the other side of our hedge. As they passed the thin bits I glimpsed them clearly for a second, then they were obscured again and only became visible for another second or two as they went past the wrought-iron gate. It was surprising how many pink, wet faces turned to glance in quickly as they scurried past. I supposed that they'd seen our removal-van two days earlier and knew that a new family had arrived. I quite liked being the object of such curiosity. Nobody in our Birmingham street had cared a hoot about us except those we'd become friends with over the years. Here it seemed that just about everybody was interested to see what we were like. If it had been a fine day I'd have hung around in the front garden all morning and maybe spoken to one or two passers-by, but, as it was, I just caught flashes of people and that's the most they saw of me.

Suddenly I saw an unmistakable little stick-like figure darting jerkily along the pavement. I was sure it was Cora as it went past two bare patches of hedge and I focused sharply on the gate to be absolutely certain. When she reached it she seemed to hesitate, as if she thought she might open it and come up to the front door. But then, without seeing me, she changed her mind and carried on past the house. I struggled with the window but couldn't open it or I'd have stuck my head out and called her back. I settled down again, and thought it was a pity I'd missed the chance of seeing

her again, when suddenly she reappeared and went through
exactly the same performance as before, of hesitating then
darting off. After that I pushed and shoved and banged at
the window till I managed to get it up a few inches, and
then I sat in a whistling draught, all ready to shout out at
her if she passed a third time. But she didn't.

Later in the morning Mother made coffee in the kitchen
for herself and Mrs. Briggs and Father, and orange juice for
the boys and me. We all sat round the table together and
Mother was comparatively cheerful and said things were
going ahead very speedily upstairs and we'd all be sleeping
in our own bedrooms that night. Then I told her that Cora
Ravenwing had walked past the house twice but I hadn't
been able to attract her attention.

"That's a pity," Mother said. "But you'll have plenty of
time to get to know her. You don't have to rush things."

Mrs. Briggs tapped her cigarette into her saucer and said:
"If I might advise . . ."

"Oh, do," said Mother affably. "You've already been such
a help."

"Well, it isn't my way to interfere, but I know how
difficult it is when you don't know your way round a place,
like," said Mrs. Briggs, looking really pleased that Mother
was so willing to listen. I didn't like the way she seemed
to be in charge, but Mother told me later that she wasn't
really taking us over and that she and Father would only
do what they wanted to do in the end, whatever Mrs. Briggs
"advised". "Nonetheless, dear," Mother said, "it is very
helpful to have someone around like that to tell you what's
what if you're new to a place."

Mrs. Briggs carried on: "That Ravenwing girl . . ." she
said. "Now, if I was you I'd keep any daughter of mine
well away from her."

"Oh?" said Father, who'd been reading the paper up until that point.

"A bad lot," said Mrs. Briggs. "That's the long and the short of it. A bad lot. You'll find everyone feels the same about her. Now I wouldn't speak bad of anyone and I won't say more. But . . ." She leaned across to my mother. "Just a word to you, dear," she said. "Keep your girl away from that one. Everybody else does. Far the best."

I began to protest and ask why, but Mother frowned and glared and said: "That'll do, Becky . . . Now, I think there's just time for another hour before lunch. That should break the back of it." There was a lot of scraping of chairs as everyone got up and that marked the close of the conversation.

The boys and I went back to the front room and I waited vigilantly for Cora, but she didn't come back. Mrs. Briggs went at lunchtime and Mother and she discussed terms of employment in the hall as she left. I couldn't hear quite what was said but, by the tones of voice, I concluded Mother had the last word that time. I was pleased. Certainly, after that first morning, Mrs. Briggs rarely again seemed quite as outspoken and opinionated on *every* topic under the sun. Mother and she became very happy and settled with each other, even friendly in a restricted sort of way, but I never again thought that she had the advantage over Mother in our own home. I hadn't liked that; I had been alarmed to see a complete stranger walk in and seem to take us all over. Mother always laughed at me for this strange notion, but I never forgot that first impression I'd had of Mrs. Briggs.

Over lunch I asked Mother and Father if they really wanted me to stay away from Cora Ravenwing. I said: "It seems a pity when she's the very first person I've met and she's been so friendly to me."

Father said: "If she seems all right to you, Becky, that's the main thing. I don't think Mrs. Briggs's opinion counts on all matters." He laughed and said to Jo: "Keep that under your hat, Jo-Jo." Then he looked across at Mother and whispered over Jo's head: "That'll be the first thing he regales your Mrs. Briggs with when she comes on Thursday—'My daddy says . . .'"

Mother laughed too and ruffled Jo's head as he bent over his plate. "I don't think he's heard a word," she said.

Chapter 3 ❧ The Graveyard

It didn't take us long after that to get the house organized, and by the end of the first week I felt as if we'd been living there for a month. On the first fine day Cora reappeared and we wandered round the village together. On various occasions she showed me the way to the school and the common and the few local shops. She continued to be very awkward and evasive whenever I asked her anything about herself but seemed perfectly content for me to talk non-stop so, as time went by, she learned all there was to learn about the Stokeses. I told her how I wanted to be a writer when I grew up and how I'd already written lots of poems and short stories. "I've started two proper books, too," I said. "But I haven't finished either of them. It takes ages."

"My mother used to write . . ." said Cora. Then she broke off and said instead: "There's a girl at school who writes, too."

"Who's that?" I asked. "Is she one of your friends? I'd love to meet her."

"She's called Hermione Phillips. She's thin, like me . . . only people think *she's* beautiful. She writes poetry about nature. I don't think it's any good but everyone else thinks it's wonderful."

"Don't you like her?"

"No. She's stuck-up. The Phillipses are rich—they don't talk to the likes of me."

I felt embarrassed. Certainly I had gathered that Cora didn't come from a rich family. For one thing she spoke with a sort of local accent which sounded all right to me but couldn't be called "posh". In addition, her clothes were a bit scruffy and she never boasted of or produced any major possessions such as a family car or a bicycle. She hadn't really told me anything about herself at all. I still didn't know where she lived. When I asked her she just pointed vaguely in whatever direction it was and said: "Over there."

I said: "Look, Cora, will you tell me a bit about yourself? What do you mean 'the likes of me'? Who are your friends, anyway? If Hermione Phillips isn't, who is?"

"I haven't got any friends," said Cora. "Unless you . . . Will you be my friend?"

"Of course," I said without thinking twice. "We already are friends, aren't we? But why haven't you got any friends? Everyone's got at least one friend."

"I haven't," said Cora. "I've never had one."

I asked her how long she'd lived in Okefield and she said she'd been there all her life. I was very puzzled. "And in all that time," I said, "you haven't had a single friend?"

"Not really. Mrs. Briggs, she's the woman that comes to help your mother cleaning, she was very kind to me when I was tiny but I don't see anything of her now."

"Mrs. Briggs!"

"She nursed me when my mother died. She'd had a baby about the same time, but it died, so she took me in till I was about eight months."

"Mrs. Briggs had a baby . . .?"

"Yes. The same birthday as mine practically. But she was quite old to have a baby then. My dad said *she* ought to have died, not my mum. But it was her baby that died— She had grown-up children; it wasn't her first."

I sat down on a boulder. It was late afternoon and we were ambling round the common. I had been about to suggest going home, but now it looked as if Cora was ready to tell some of the secrets she'd been holding back and I didn't want to interrupt her. She might take weeks to get to this stage again. I patted the boulder. "Cora, sit down," I said, gently. "Tell me about your mother. I didn't know she'd died."

Cora sat down. "That's a wonder," she said. "I thought Mrs. Briggs would have told you all about that."

"Not a word," I said, keeping quiet about what Mrs. Briggs *had* actually said.

"There's not much to say about Mum," said Cora. She didn't seem sad particularly, just matter-of-fact. "She died just after I was born. I don't know why, exactly, just something that can happen to women after they have a baby. It happened to her."

"Poor her," I said, "and poor you. It must be very hard without a mother." I could hardly think of anything worse, but I didn't want to upset Cora by showing the extent of my horror at such a predicament.

"It's not so bad," said Cora in her usual flat voice. Her face was equally expressionless. It was almost impossible ever to know what she was thinking; she never smiled but she never looked particularly downcast either. "I've never known anything different. It would be nasty for you if your mother died right now, because she means something to you, but mine never meant anything to me."

I was chilled by these remarks—the suggestion that my own mother could possibly die "right now", and the terrible, empty space Cora had revealed in her own life. I wanted to argue with her and say that of course her mother meant something to her even if she'd never known her. Surely she must be curious about what she'd been like. But, for fear of hurting her by my prying insistence, I thought it best to follow her lead and make light of the whole thing.

"I see what you mean," I said. "So Mrs. Briggs took over while you were tiny—and then did you go back to live with your father?"

"Yes. Mrs. Briggs was my wet-nurse—that's what they call it—till her husband walked out on her. Then I went back to Dad."

"Good heavens! What an awful time! Poor Mrs. Briggs! Baby dying, husband deserting her." I felt a pang of sympathy for Mrs. Briggs despite my instinctive dislike of her.

"You don't need to feel too sorry for her," said Cora sharply.

"Oh, I don't know. That seems hard . . ."

"You just don't. That's all." Cora jumped up, shaking her fringe out of her eyes. "Let's go."

On our way home from the common we passed St. Matthew's Church. The reddening evening sun brought out a warmth in the stone and gleamed on the clock face on the square tower. The graveyard was grassy and green, dotted here and there with the bumps and mounds of unmarked graves. There was also the usual variety of headstones, old and new, planted haphazardly between dark yew trees. Not a bad place to be buried if that's what it had to come to.

"Let's go in," said Cora. "I love it. My mum's buried here."

I wasn't very keen. The sun was dropping fast; faint breezes were stirring; graveyards frightened me. "I'm late already," I protested.

"Come on," said Cora, pushing open the gate. I felt the initiative passing, for the first time, from me to her. "Come on!" She went in and beckoned me to follow. She seemed to come alive, for the first time since I had met her, dancing and pirouetting over the grass with unexpected grace. "Come on, Becky! Come and see!" she called back to me as I hesitated. But she didn't wait for me; she disappeared behind the church; she knew I'd follow.

I didn't want to go in. I didn't like walking over the grass, nice as it looked from the road. I kept thinking I was walking over corpses and of all the curses and bad luck I'd be bringing down on myself as a result. The graves were so close-packed that it was quite difficult to pick one's way round the marked ones, never mind the unmarked lumps and bumps. Round the corner I came upon Cora sitting cross-legged beside a simple headstone. At its foot was a small rectangular flower-bed planted with rose bushes. "Look!" said Cora. "She's here."

I felt quite shaky as I read the headstone. "Myra Raven-wing, dear wife of Ernest and mother of Cora, 1920–45. Rest easy." I sat down silently while, for the first time, Cora chattered on.

"She's got such a lovely grave, hasn't she? Dad organized it all. He works here, he's sexton—here and at St. Margaret's in Overoke. Look, I'm making a daisy-chain. She loved flowers. She wrote sort of nature diaries, all about the

different flowers of the different seasons and what they
looked like and what they could be used for—dyes, medicines. My middle name's Rose, you know. Dad thought of
that. Then he planted roses here for her. It's a link between
us, isn't it? I like that. Sometimes I lie right down here
beside her and I talk to her and sing to her and tell her
what flowers are out. She hears me, I'm certain. So I have
got a mum too, you see. Not like yours, but real all the
same."

She turned her black-eyed stare on me. Her face was
bright and smiling, chirpy almost. The sun was nearly gone;
it was getting cool; soon it would start to get dark. "I must
go, Cora," I said. "Mummy'll be wondering."

"Don't go yet," she pleaded. "Wait for the church bells.
See, it's nearly half-past." So we sat and waited for the
bells and when they sounded I jumped out of my skin because they were so loud at such close quarters. But, by the
end, my ears had accustomed themselves to the full, rich
tones and I was glad we'd stayed. The predictable chiming
of the ancient clock somehow dispelled a sudden fear that
Cora's strange, feverish chatter had roused in me.

While I still felt calm, I rose to my feet. "Come on,
Cora," I said. "Time to move. Won't your father be expecting you?" I knew my mother would be getting agitated
by this time.

"He'll be at the pub," said Cora. "Look, I live in that
cottage over there. He leaves the door unlocked for me."
The cottage was just through the hedge from the graveyard. It looked small and dark.

I thought of my own home, full of light and warmth and
people waiting for me. "Oh, Cora . . ." I began. But what
was the point of saying, "How dreadful!" or, "How sad!"?
I just said: "What a pretty little house!"

Then I had to dash. Cora ran with me all the way home and left me at the gate to wander back again to the empty cottage.

Inside, my mother was relieved and enraged at the sight of me. "What time do you call this?" she scolded. "Just you get up to bed at once and be glad your father's not home yet or goodness knows what he'd say." I went straight up and got ready for bed and when I was writing up my diary she came in and sat on the bed. "Where were you, Becky?" she asked wearily.

"Just with Cora," I said.

"Oh, that Cora!" she said. "I don't know—perhaps Mrs. Briggs was right—she's leading you into bad ways. You've never been so late before."

"Oh, it wasn't Cora's fault," I said. And I told her about Cora's mother and about her lonely life in the cottage. But, for some reason, I didn't tell her then about Mrs. Briggs's part in her story or about our visit to the church-yard.

"Dear, dear! Poor little thing!" said Mother. "Don't some people have it hard?" She seemed as moved as I had been by Cora's plight and after she'd kissed me and turned my light out she wandered off downstairs murmuring, "Poor little mite! What chance does she have?"

All the same, after that I began to notice an ambivalence in Mother's attitude to Cora. Certainly she had every sympathy with her, deprived of a mother's love and neglected, as she saw it, by the father, but, at the same time, I suspected that she didn't want me to befriend Cora too exclusively. Perhaps Mrs. Briggs's words had made an impression on her, despite her own judgement, or perhaps she feared that if Cora became too frequent a visitor at our house she would find herself, whether she wanted it or not,

becoming almost a substitute mother. She'd say things like:
"Cora's fine, Becky. I've nothing against the child at all—
I'm very sorry for her—but you must have other friends
too. There's no point tying yourself up completely before
you've even met the others."

I thought it very strange myself that Cora had no other
friends. She didn't seem all that bad to me. She did have a
musty smell about her and she wasn't very pretty, but lots
of us weren't, and she was often rather dreary company,
but she was a good listener. The most off-putting thing
about her as far as I was concerned was the strange vitality
that came over her in the graveyard. It was alarming to
see her transformed from her usual drab lifelessness to such
lightness and brightness amongst all those corpses. At her
insistence I went with her to the graveyard several times,
and I tried to be brave and told myself that this was Cora
at her best and that if only she could bring all this vivacity
and sweetness out of the graveyard and into the rest of her
life her problems would be solved. But she never seemed
able to do that. This side of her personality was reserved
solely for her mother's graveside. When we were there she
spoke vividly of how her mother had been so beautiful, so
at one with nature and its ways, almost a fairy woman.
"I'd like to dance like a fairy," she'd say and skip round
and round the grave with surprising agility and speed.

One day, when we were sitting there, she said: "That
Hermione Phillips writes dreadful poetry. It's just phoney.
She writes about nature all the time and she knows nothing
about it at all. She doesn't know the names of the flowers
or where they grow or anything. My mum knew all that
sort of thing. And she could paint. You must see her diaries
one day when you come to our house . . ."

"You do spend a lot of time thinking about her, don't

you, Cora?" I said quietly. "Remember you told me at first you never gave her a thought?"

"Mmmm," said Cora. "But I don't always. It's just when I'm here I almost want to *be* her. I think how marvellous it would be if she could somehow come alive again in me. Dad would love it. But he says I take after him—he says I'm nothing like her at all."

"Is he nice to you?" I asked.

"Yes, he's very good to me. He loves me. But he's sad about her all the time. Sometimes I think it's my fault she's dead. If she hadn't had me . . ."

"You mustn't think that, Cora," I protested. "It wasn't your fault at all. Nobody's to blame."

"That's what Dad says," she said in a low voice. "But it's a fact all the same. If I wasn't here she still would be and it's obvious which of us Dad would rather have."

"Don't be silly," I said desperately. "He'd rather have both of you. Apart from that it's not a question of choice."

"Mum says that," murmured Cora, staring at the soil of the flower-bed. "I've *heard* her say that."

Again I felt a shiver of fear run up my back. I glanced round to check that we were on our own, no sudden appearance of anyone else, real or imaginary. "I get the creeps when you talk like that, Cora," I said.

Then she turned her bright, black eyes on me and reached out a hand, perhaps to comfort me, I don't know. Her outstretched arm was silhouetted against the sun like a black stick with five bony prongs on the end. It seemed to be coming for me. "Don't touch me!" I screamed. I leapt up and ran for my life, helter-skelter over all the graves, through the gate and off down the lane to the village. I didn't stop till I burst in through our own back door.

"Becky! Becky! What's happened?" gasped Mother,

folding her big warm arms round me. But I couldn't speak for panting and trembling. She sat me down and made sweet tea. As I sipped it and began to recover, she said: "Did someone hurt you, darling?"

"No, no," I said, seeing the extent of her anxiety. "It was Cora."

"Cora!" she exclaimed. "What on earth's Cora done?"

"Nothing really, I don't think," I said. "I just felt scared out of my wits—I thought she was a witch or a skeleton raised from the dead." Just talking about it brought the scene vividly back to me and I quaked with fright again.

Joseph looked up from his building-set on the floor. "Is Cora a witch?" he asked. "A real witch? Can she do spells?"

"Be quiet, Jo, and don't talk rubbish," snapped Mother. Then she turned to me again. "Now look, Becky," she said. "You're just letting your imagination run wild. Cora is a perfectly ordinary, rather lonely, child. She's got quite enough to contend with without you using her tragic little life to frighten yourself to death with. Where is she now? Have you just run off and left her somewhere?"

"She's in the graveyard," I said, "talking to the spirit of her mother who's buried there, if you want to know." I said all this in a rush of hatred for Mother because she was scolding me and blaming me and accusing me of somehow exploiting Cora's misfortune for the sake of morbid titillation. Then I started to sob and I told Mother all about our visits to the graveside and Cora's odd behaviour there and how it had always given me the shivers despite my efforts to view it calmly and rationally.

From time to time Mother glanced at Jo to see if he was listening, but he was absorbed in an attempt to construct a crane. Dory was upstairs in his cot, having an afternoon rest. "I'm sorry I was sharp with you, darling," she said when I'd finished. "Really I was just relieved that it was only Cora who'd frightened you. When you came rushing in I didn't know what had happened. But I do think you've been seeing rather a lot of Cora recently and it seems to be getting you down. It's sad when we meet people who're lonely and friendless, and we want to make it up to them somehow. But we can't always. Just be a normal friend to her, Becky. Don't try to make her happy overnight; don't take her over; don't think you can compensate for everything she's missed. Just see her now and then. By all means be open and friendly but make an effort to make other friends too."

I could see that she was right. I had been thinking I could organize Cora, change her ways, help her to be happier. But during the graveyard visits she almost seemed to be taking me over, compelling me to spectate her strange transformation and become a witness to her communications with her dead mother. It had finally preyed on my mind to the extent that I was just about ready to believe she was in touch with the supernatural, with her black, piercing eyes, her bony, skeletal arms and legs and her weird, gleeful dancing there amongst the dead.

Chapter 4 ❧ Stansfield House

IT WAS ALL TO THE GOOD, THEREFORE, THAT A DAY OR TWO
after that Mother went to her first meeting of the Mothers'
Union in the church hall and met Hermione Phillips's
mother. She came home brimming with satisfaction and
told me she'd solved my problems already. "I've had a
really good afternoon," she said, taking Dory on her knee
and sitting down on the wicker chair in the kitchen to tell
Jo and me her news. "First we had a pleasant talk about
flower arrangement and then we sat at tables for afternoon
tea. The vicar's wife made a point of introducing me to
several people and I finally shared a table with a Mrs.
Phillips . . ."

"Were there cakes?" asked Jo.

"Er—yes, a few, and biscuits. Now, this Mrs. . . ."

"What kind?" asked Jo.

"Swiss rolls. Now, Jo, let me tell Becky something . . ."
Jo slid off his chair and wandered off into the garden.
Mother looked guilty. "Has he been all right while I've

been away? Do you need a baby-sitter, Becky, or can you really manage the boys?"

"Course I can. Not at night—but I can during the day. Dory's only just woken up, anyway. Jo's fine—he's just bored. What were you going to tell me?"

"Well, Mrs. Phillips has a daughter, Hermione, at Okington School and she's your age, so you'll probably be in the same class. She's suggested that you go there for tea tomorrow so the two of you can meet."

"Just me? Or all of us?" I felt nervous of going by myself.

"She asked us all but I thought it'd be silly to take the boys. There's nothing there for them and they'd just interrupt and probably spoil things. So I said you'd go on your own."

"Oh, Mummy! What if she doesn't like me? Oh, I really think it'd be better if we all went . . ."

"Well, I don't. Honestly, Becky, I was thinking of you. I'd quite like to see Sylvia Phillips again, but I just thought we'd all cramp your style. Now, it really is time you began to stand on your own feet a bit. It'll only be a couple of hours or so. And I'm sure Hermione will be awfully nice—her mother is."

The next afternoon it was sunny again; we were having a beautiful summer that year. I put on one of my two non-school summer dresses and hoped that Hermione and her mother would like me in it. Mother said she thought it'd be more suitable than shorts for meeting them the first time. It was Saturday and she said she'd walk the boys round to the Phillipses' with me just to show me the way. Father would stay behind to tidy up the garden. I said I thought I'd look a bit babyish being delivered at the door but Mother said there wouldn't be a chance of them being seen. I saw what she meant when we arrived. The Phillipses' house, which was actually quite near ours, was out of sight from the village street, up a private drive bordered by rhododendrons. There were huge stone gateposts on either side, though the gates had long since been taken away, and a discreet wooden sign to one side bore the inscription: "Stansfield House."

"Mummy! You didn't say they were grand . . ."

Mother smiled. She had known I'd falter at this point and that's why she'd come. "They're not that grand," she said, laughing at my dismay. "They've just got a bit of money, that's all. Now, in you go, love, and have a good time. You look very nice."

She gave me a prod and I started off up the sandy drive, which curved away to the right so that Mother and the boys couldn't stare after me for long. I was glad; I felt very awkward and shy and didn't want to be watched. I half expected an irate gardener to step out of the bushes and order me off the premises. Instead, a girl on a red bicycle suddenly wobbled into sight along the bumpy track. I stopped and she stopped and said: "Are you Rebecca Stokes?"

"Yes."

"I'm Hermione Phillips." She got off the bike and turned it round and we carried on up the drive together in silence.

"What a lovely house!" I said when it came into view. It was enormous—three storeys high, with an arched front door and huge windows on either side. To right and left were low outhouses—stables, garages, greenhouses, As we got nearer, the rhododendron drive gave way to a stony forecourt where a land rover and a sports car were parked.

"Are you one of a very huge family?" I asked.

"Five children." She parked her bicycle and pushed the

heavy oak door open with her shoulder. "I've got four brothers. I'm the youngest."

I followed her into a small lobby and we were instantly confronted by an inner door which she pushed open, using most of the strength of her small frame. She was very slender and fair, with masses of tight curls all over her head. I didn't feel very pretty in comparison and thought I should be doing all the pushing and shoving at these massive doors. She led me across a big panelled hall with a polished floor dotted with foreign-looking rugs; the stairs, with their carved banisters, ran diagonally up the far wall.

"Mummy, I've got Rebecca," she called, and took me into a wide, bright kitchen. Mrs. Phillips was reaching tea things down from the Welsh dresser and laying the table for quite a number. I was horrified. This was all going to be a tremendous ordeal—four big brothers and Hermione and her mother and father all at once.

"Hello, Rebecca," said Mrs. Phillips. "How nice to meet you, dear. Sit down for a minute till you feel more at home. How are you liking life in our little village?"

"Very much, thank you, Mrs. Phillips," I said, all pink with confusion. I sat down on one of the pine chairs as she'd said, but wished I hadn't as Hermione wandered round the room restlessly and seemed to want to be elsewhere.

"When's tea, Mummy?"

"Another half hour or so, dear. Daddy's taken the car in for a service and he's walking back with Hector and James. Shall we wait till they get back?"

"All right." But Hermione tossed her head as if that idea didn't suit her at all. Then she began to bite a thumb nail.

"What is it, sweetheart?" said Mrs. Phillips gently. "Do you want to show Rebecca the garden?"

"Mmmm. I was just thinking it'd be difficult for us to talk with the boys and Daddy milling round cracking jokes. Couldn't we have tea on our own?"

Mrs. Phillips was so understanding then. She didn't insist on our fitting in with her arrangements but suggested making us a little picnic tea and, in no time, Hermione and I were out through the back door with sandwiches and orange juice and meringues in a basket. I thought disloyally of how my own mother would have put her foot down and made us wait in the kitchen. "Your mother's really nice," I said to Hermione.

"I know," she said. She looked at me intently and paused in the middle of the lawn. "Do you think I'm spoiled?"

"Oh, I've no idea," I said. "I suppose you might be—being the youngest and the only girl. But I didn't mean that. I just thought it was kind of her to make us a picnic."

"Yes, it was," agreed Hermione, "but I didn't really think twice about it till you mentioned it."

We walked across the grass towards some big trees at the end of the garden. A swing and a rope ladder hung from the thick branches of one of them. The sun shone down on us. I felt warm and happy in my light cotton frock with my new friend. "It's perfect here, Hermione."

"Do you think so?" she said. "I'm glad. I love it too. We're so lucky. Do let me show you the whole garden—it's really beautiful."

It was—big and beautiful. Beyond the trees there was a sunken rose garden with crazy-paving pathways running between the beds. Then there was a spinney of silver birch trees and finally a paddock where two horses were grazing. We sat on the gate watching them and trying to tempt them over with bunches of grass, but they were content to stay where they were, eating the grass at their feet and flicking the flies away with their long tails.

"They're not ours," said Hermione. "Someone from the village rents the paddock and stables from Daddy. He says he's pleased to have them in use."

We sat in the sunshine and began to talk about schools— the one I'd just left and Okington, where it seemed more than likely we would be form-mates next term. She told me about her two friends and the teacher we would be having and rules that were strictly upheld and lunch-time arrangements and the school uniform. She seemed to enjoy the school very much and I became quite excited at the prospect of starting there.

"It all sounds very nice," I said. "Actually I've already met someone who's probably in the same class."

"Who's that?"

"A girl called Cora Ravenwing."

"Oh *her*!" said Hermione. I waited for her to say something else but she didn't.

"She seems quite nice," I persisted, "but difficult to get to know and a bit odd in some ways."

"Mmmm," said Hermione. "Well, I don't know her really. She is in our class but . . . Are you *very* friendly with her?"

"Not very," I said. "We haven't been here all that long, so I couldn't know her very well yet. But she's always coming round for me. Actually, she seems a bit lonely. She says she hasn't got any friends at all—is that right?"

"I suppose it is," said Hermione.

"Why not?"

Hermione didn't seem to want to answer. She shrugged and screwed up her eyes as if it was a terribly difficult question. Then she jumped down from the gate and said:

"Look. I want to show you something else, something very special. It's a secret place of my own. Let's have our tea there. And I'll tell you a bit about Cora Ravenwing, though I don't really know if I should."

Not far from the paddock was a thicket of slender new saplings covered with silky pale green leaves. Hermione dropped to her knees and began to crawl along a little passage. "Isn't it super?" she said, "I call it Paradise—that's from *What Katy Did*. Have you read it? She had a special place of her own called that." We crawled along for quite a way and then came out into a tiny, circular clearing. "Isn't it odd," said Hermione, "how none of the saplings have rooted themselves just here? I don't understand it at all. But it makes a perfect, secluded little den."

"It's lovely," I agreed. Above us the sky was bright blue and all around the saplings encircled us with a fluttering leafy screen.

"I write poetry here," said Hermione, stroking a leaf between finger and thumb. "I write quite a lot of nature poetry. I love nature. A lot of lines seem to come into my head when I lie in here alone on days like this and listen to the birds and watch the leaves. And, if you really look around you, you see such brilliant details—Look at this moss, for instance. It grows round the roots of nearly all the saplings but you don't notice it at first."

I didn't say that I'd seen it all the way along the passage-way as we'd crawled in. But I remembered Cora's scorn of Hermione's verse. "I've tried to write poetry myself," I said, hesitating to invade her domain.

"How super, Rebecca! I've been dying to meet someone who was really interested. My other friends at school think it's a bit arty-crafty." She seemed genuinely pleased and wanted me to recite a specimen of my work.

"I'll let you read some of it next time I see you," I said, delaying an embarrassing moment. "And I'd like to read some of yours too."

It was the discovery of this shared interest that seemed to decide Hermione that I was really all right. She'd been tense till then, trying to sum me up, but now she seemed to accept me. We sat up and divided the picnic and, as we ate, she began to tell me about Cora Ravenwing.

"She's very unpopular at school and in the village generally," she said. "None of the mothers like her, so nobody ever talks to her much or asks her home to tea or anything like that."

"Why not?"

"Well, we're not supposed to talk about it all really. You won't say I told you . . . ?"

"No, no. I won't."

"Well, there are stories about her. People say she's peculiar . . ."

"Peculiar!"

"Well, they say she was born odd." Hermione was in difficulties, it seemed, not wanting to say more than she had to, but I was insistent.

"What do you mean—'odd'?"

"Oh, dear," said Hermione. "I shouldn't say. I promised Mummy I wouldn't gossip about her . . ."

"*Please* tell me," I pleaded.

"Well, they say she killed her mother," said Hermione suddenly. And once she'd said this much she just went on and spilled out the whole weird tale in a rush. "Her mother was apparently a very beautiful gypsy sort of woman—very young. She and Mr. Ravenwing came to live in Okefield a year before Cora was born and everyone really took to Mrs. Ravenwing. The husband was a bit quiet and retiring

but people just assumed that went with his job somehow—
he's a grave-digger. And Mrs. Ravenwing always seemed so
happy that people were sure he must be very nice really.
She used to wander round in all weathers, singing all the
time and gathering flowers, which she used to press and
paint and make medicines out of and all sorts. She did all
the floral decorations in the church and used to do marvellous displays for weddings and very pretty funeral
wreaths. She used wild flowers nearly all the time and even
in winter she managed to find evergreens or attractive
twigs—things you wouldn't usually notice."

"Cora did tell me she was a great naturalist. Apparently
she wrote diaries about plants and things."

"I didn't know that," said Hermione. "But lots of people
actually bought her flower paintings. We've got two up in
the house . . . Anyway, she seemed to be in perfect health
all the time she was expecting Cora, absolutely blossoming
and looking forward to having her baby. Then, the next
thing that was heard, she was dead—died in childbirth at
home—no midwife there or anything—just Mr. Ravenwing
and the new baby."

"Well, that's very sad—but I can't see why it's made all
the mothers dislike Cora."

"I know. It does seem queer, but there's lots more to it
than that. Mummy tried to explain it all to me ages ago,
when there were an awful lot of strange rumours circulat-
ing about how Cora was turning out, and they seemed to
fit in with the dreadful things that Mrs. Briggs had said
about her when she was a baby."

"Ooh, that Mrs. Briggs!" I said. "She says an awful lot
sometimes. I don't really like her very much—she helps
Mummy in the house, you know."

"She comes here too sometimes. We've got Horti, actually; she lives up on the attic floor—she's our *au pair*. She does quite a lot of cleaning, but sometimes Mummy gets Mrs. Briggs in to lend a hand. She frightens me, you know; she gets so carried away about certain things, including Cora, that I just go away rather than listen. Mummy says it's mainly hysterical nonsense anyway. She doesn't like me to hear. Horti can't stand her either; she won't work in the same room. All the same, I sometimes wonder if Mummy does half believe some of the stories against Cora, because she certainly doesn't want me to have anything to do with her."

"Well, I think Mrs. Briggs is absolutely foul," I said. "saying horrible things about a tiny baby and trying to make everyone hate her."

"She took Cora in, you know," said Hermione. "She had a new baby herself just about the same time as Cora was born. But it died—never really had a chance, apparently—there was something wrong with its heart. The doctor thought it might help her a bit if she could mother another baby, so he arranged for her to have Cora. It solved Mr. Ravenwing's problem about what to do with Cora, too."

"You'd think she'd be specially close to Cora then . . ."

"I know. But something went dreadfully wrong. It was to do with her husband, I think. When Cora was about eight months old he suddenly up and left Mrs. Briggs, and she took to blaming it all on Cora."

"How on earth . . .? How could it have been Cora's fault?"

"I don't suppose it was. But Mrs. Briggs just seemed to turn on her—said she'd been a screaming brat from start to finish and that she'd driven her husband away . . ."

"But Mrs. Briggs has still got a husband—I've seen him— a little, thin, pale old man . . ."

"I know. He came creeping back again after a bit. But not before Mrs. Briggs had dumped Cora back on her father's doorstep at dead of night. She left her there, wrapped up in an old black-out. The milkman found her screaming her head off at crack of dawn. There was the most almighty fuss, apparently, with police and everything. But Mrs. Briggs wasn't arrested because they said she was temporarily deranged because of losing her own baby. And her husband came back then—I suppose he felt to blame."

"He looks such a weak, ill sort of man."

"Mrs. Briggs has always hounded him to death—that's one theory. Bullied the life out of him. But Mummy says he's never had good health. It's hard to know what Mrs. Briggs is like really. Anyway Mr. Ravenwing took Cora back and has looked after her ever since. She has more or less been brought up in the graveyard, Mummy says. First she used to lie there in her pram, watching her father digging graves and gardening, and later she used to potter round behind him, playing in half-dug graves and so on. Don't you think that's unnatural, somehow? People said she was always appearing at funerals, creeping up during the graveside service and peering out from behind gravestones. And when the mourners went away she used to dance round the new grave and fiddle about with the wreaths and sprays, pinning the flowers in her hair and just seeming to delight in it all."

"I must say I think that side of her can be a bit frightening," I said and I told Hermione about the times I'd been in the graveyard with Cora. "But I think it's understandable after the kind of life she's had."

Hermione looked surprised. "Oh, well," she said, "there's more to it than that. There's some sort of badness in her, you know, even if she isn't absolutely evil, as Mrs. Briggs says. She's not like the rest of us. It's definitely true." She seemed to want to persuade me, to have the matter closed and my decision safely made in favour of repudiating Cora completely. "Mrs. Briggs is quite sure she's a changeling. She thinks Mrs. Ravenwing couldn't possibly have given birth to a creature like that and that Cora was somehow substituted."

"Oh, that's completely mad!" I said. "I'm surprised people have put up with that sort of wicked nonsense. It sounds as if she just blames Cora for simply being alive when her child isn't—but that's no excuse for persecuting her."

Hermione became a little distant when she saw I wasn't impressed with her horror story. "Oh, well—you'll see," she said. "It probably sounds crazy to you because you're a newcomer here. But when you've lived here longer you'll see what I mean. I'm not saying Cora *is* a changeling; I'm not saying anything about her, one way or the other; I'm just explaining the background because you asked."

"Oh, I know, Hermione," I said quickly. "I did want to know. I'm sorry to seem rude . . ."

"You'll find the others at school won't like it if you're friendly with Cora."

"Well, I'm not particularly. In fact she scared me out of my wits the last time I saw her."

"There you are, you see. And she's been terribly naughty, you know. She used to steal—people's flowers mainly. She used to sneak into gardens at night and pick whole bunches, even dig plants up by the roots. People never got the police because they were sorry for her. And, in any case, Mrs. Briggs's stories about her being evil used to scare some of the old villagers and they thought if they crossed her she might bring heaven knows what sort of curse down on their heads."

"Don't you think she might just have been terribly lonely and wanting the flowers for her mother's grave or something?" I said. "She must have been awfully young when she did all these things."

"Well—I know," said Hermione. "But it got worse, actually. Not so long ago she just about poisoned Susan Spenser's little brother in his pram in their very own garden. He'd been awfully poorly with measles and was taking a long time to recover, but he was picking up at last and then in sneaked Cora and fed him some spoonfuls of a concoction she'd brewed up from roots."

"Heavens! That was really frightful!" I said. "She's funny about sneaking around people's gardens, isn't she? We found her in ours—but she said she was only looking."

"Well, just think. It could have been *your* baby brother if you'd been here a year or two ago."

"What happened to the baby?"

"Oh, he's all right. He recovered. But he might not have done. He had to go to hospital. Luckily Mrs. Spenser caught Cora red-handed or they might not have known what was wrong with him."

"Gosh . . ."

"Yes, you see. As it is, the Spensers have never spoken to Cora or her father again. And, as we're very friendly with the Spensers, we haven't either. I don't think anybody has very much really."

"I can understand how people feel about that," I said. "At the same time, Cora was only trying to cure the baby, don't you think?"

"She nearly killed him," said Hermione crossly. "That's what counts."

I could see that our new friendship was going to fizzle out even before it started if I persisted in arguing and taking Cora's side, and it seemed foolish to jeopardize the relationship with Hermione when my last encounter with Cora had been so terrifying in any case. I also remembered my mother's advice that, even if I wanted to be friendly with Cora and help her, I didn't need to cut myself off from everyone else. "You're probably right," I said quickly. "The whole story is just so unusual it's hard to understand it all."

Hermione was appeased. "I expect it is. We're not really supposed to talk about it, anyway. Mummy'd be cross with me for telling you. She says that even if we can't forget and forgive we can at least keep quiet."

"Let's not talk about Cora any more, then," I said. "I don't want to do anything to offend your mother."

We stretched out in the sunny little glade and ate our sticky meringues and recited poems to each other, not our own, but ones we'd learned at school. I enjoyed myself tremendously and thought Hermione's recitations superbly executed, her tones of voice and facial expressions so aptly assumed. I thought she was very beautiful. At last we heard a faint "Coo-eee" in the distance. "That's Mummy," said Hermione. "She must want us to go in." We jumped up and brushed the crumbs from our frocks. Then down we went on our hands and knees again and crawled our way out of Paradise.

Back at the house I encountered almost the whole family, but it was less of an ordeal than I'd expected because I knew that Hermione and I were friends. Her father was a big cheerful man. He was wearing a green tweed suit with plus fours. Hermione saw me looking at his legs and whispered, "He just wears those at weekends—he's a city gent really!" He shook my hand and asked lots of questions about me and Mother and Father. He even asked how old they were and what job Father had, which seemed a bit nosy, but I was flattered at his interest and told him all he wanted to know. Hermione's oldest brother, Hector, was there but he didn't say much—just nodded and smiled and stroked a big yellow retriever which was resting its head on his knee. The next brother, Angus, was off somewhere playing cricket, but two more boys, James and Tom, were sitting at the table and they started teasing Hermione as soon as we came in. "Been reading her your poems then, Herm?" asked Tom, and James whispered to me: "Don't forget to tell her how marvellous they are. She thinks she's very good, you know."

Hermione looked so pink and hurt that I spoke out quite firmly. "No, she hasn't read me her poems yet, but I hope she will one day. I'm sure they're good."

Mr. Phillips looked pleased with me and said: "Bravely spoken, Rebecca. These jokers need putting in their place from time to time." He'd taken Hermione on his knee and she was resting her blonde curls against his cheek. I thought how long it was since I'd sat on Father's knee and felt a pang of envy. Only Dory sat on Father's knee nowadays; even Jo wasn't encouraged in baby ways. "Are you going to take Rebecca down the drive, pet?" he murmured in her ear. "It's time she went home, you know. Her mummy'll be waiting."

I thanked Mrs. Phillips for our picnic as politely as I knew how, but she seemed busy now the others were home and hardly noticed my departure. Hermione did, though, and at the end of the drive she said: "Look, that was a really nice afternoon. I'm pleased you've come to live here. Let's meet again soon."

I said: "I've enjoyed it all too. I can't tell you how nice

it's been to meet somebody else from the school. I'll get Mummy to ring your mother and ask you to tea at our house."

Hermione went back up the private drive and I started off along the pavement to our house.

Suddenly a thin dark figure sprang out of a gateway as I passed and barred the way. It was Cora. "You've been at the Phillipses', haven't you?" she hissed. Her eyes were staring out through her fringe and her face looked pinched and hurt. "What did she tell you about me? Bad things, didn't she? Did she tell you I kill and steal? Did she tell you I'm a Devil Child? Tell me what she said."

She seized hold of my arm with her bony fingers but I wasn't frightened. I looked down at her, so skinny and agitated and lonely. "Don't be daft, Cora," I said. "She didn't say anything. Don't make a fuss."

She let go of me and jerkily scraped her hands across her face. She could have been brushing her fringe out of her eyes or dashing away tears before I saw them; I wasn't sure which. "Don't forget you're my friend, Becky." She just stood there with her head drooping down.

"Of course I won't forget."

"Why did you scream at me the other day?"

"I was scared in the graveyard. Loads of people are."

"I'm not; I love it there."

"I know—but that's because you're so used to it. You've practically been brought up there."

"Did Hermione Phillips say that?"

"Well, I suppose she did."

"You *did* talk about me then!"

"Not much."

"Did she tell you the bad things I've done? Did she tell you what Mrs. Briggs says?"

"Oh—she told me all sorts. But she wasn't terribly mean about you. She didn't say she believed it all."

"Do you believe it all, Becky?"

"No—I think it's all nonsense. I believe you've done some silly things—very naughty. But I don't believe you're evil and all that."

Cora seemed relieved. She wanted to go for a walk, but it was getting late and I had to go home. I didn't want to walk with her then, anyway. She was too sad and troubled and dark, and my mind was full of Hermione with her blonde curls, poetic visions and secret Paradise.

Chapter 5 ❦ The Gang

MOTHER WAS PLEASED THAT I'D MANAGED TO GET ON WITH Hermione. "There you are, dear," she said, "another friend for you. And there'll be lots of other nice girls in your class. I expect Hermione will introduce you one or two before term begins. We'll have her round here soon and then they'll probably ask you back."

I didn't tell Mother any of the rumours and stories I'd heard about Cora. I'd made up my own mind what I thought of those and I didn't want Mother getting worried about that particular friendship. I hoped I'd somehow be able to be friendly with everybody; perhaps I, a newcomer and complete outsider, could bridge the gap between Cora and the others. It wasn't that I felt particularly drawn to Cora at that stage—I was much more drawn to Hermione and felt challenged by her poetry and her big rich family —I just felt sorry for her; she'd never had a chance to be anything. I could imagine how I might have turned out in her shoes.

Mother did ask Hermione to tea a few days later. It was very different from my visit to Stansfield House, but Hermione loved playing with Dory and was nice to Jo too. We all had tea together in the kitchen and Dory got very silly with his food, dropping baked beans in his orange juice and spooning jelly on to the table. I could see that Mother was really quite enraged with him but Hermione was so amused and intrigued by his antics that she pretty well turned a blind eye. Jo was very shy at first; I think he was overcome by Hermione's beauty. We were all stocky and dark, while she was so light and blonde. Eventually he took it upon himself to crayon a special picture for her to take home and she was very pleased with it, which made him feel happy and proud. I was greatly relieved that she wasn't bored by the boys; I thought they might seem very tiresome and dull after her experience of four older brothers. But she said afterwards, when we went upstairs to my bedroom to be on our own, that it was lovely being the oldest for once.

She'd brought some of her poetry with her and asked if she could see some of mine. My heart was thumping as she read it and I could hardly concentrate on hers for hoping that she'd think mine at least passable. I did take in, however, that her work was very much concerned with nature —weather, flowers, birds, the seasons and their effect on one's emotions. I remembered Cora's tremendous scorn of her verses, but I didn't share it. I thought them very wise and mature. I didn't think I could ever have had the thoughts which she expressed so elegantly. I could hear her rustling through the pages of my notebook, but I didn't dare look up at her expression. Long after I'd finished reading hers I sat with lowered head, pretending still to be pondering their significance. At last she said: "You deal with much more everyday matters than I do, don't you?"

"Yes, I suppose I do really."

"Aren't our styles different?"

"Very."

"I like yours, though, Becky. They're very vivid and forth-right."

"Yours are marvellous, Hermione. So thoughtful."

"It's quite good that we're so different, don't you think? It wouldn't be so nice if we were rivals." I wondered if she thought she was streets ahead of me. She certainly didn't say so. But I thought she must be thinking that. My poems were factual descriptions of people and places, full of rhymes and square-looking stanzas. Hers seemed to drift on and on in progressions of thoughts growing out of one another. "Actually, I find rhymes very difficult. Perhaps you found mine a bit dull . . ."

"Oh, not at all. I sometimes think my own are too jingly-jangly."

We both enjoyed this sort of talk. We felt as if we were real writers discussing our craft. We speculated on what fun it would be to set ourselves the same topic to write about and see how different the end results were. We wondered if it might work to write together, with Hermione provid-ing the train of thought and me rhyming it. Our time together flew by. We didn't talk about Cora or school at all until the last minute, when I was seeing her off.

"Oh, listen. Mummy thinks it might be nice for you to meet some of my other school friends. Would you like that?"

I said I'd like it very much and she invited me to go round the next Saturday afternoon. That would be the

second Saturday in a row that I'd spent at Stansfield House.
I looked forward to it eagerly.

During the intervening days, of course, I saw Cora more
than once. I thought Mother was a bit irritated about that.
"What do you want to see so much of Cora for?" she'd ask.
"I thought you'd had enough of her. I thought she frightened
you half to death."

"I was stupid that evening and very unfair to Cora. She
was jolly hurt; she couldn't think what she'd done."

"Oh, I see. Well, this is a change of heart, I must say!
You seemed to want to get rid of her badly enough a week
or so ago. In any case, I don't want you messing around
in the churchyard. That's where people bury their dead; it's
a consecrated, holy place, not a playground."

"We haven't been there for ages."

"Good. Well, that's all I'm saying—do not go poking
around amongst the graves. It's not healthy and people
don't like it." She stamped on the Hoover button and roared
off over the carpets, deaf to my protestations.

It was this sort of attitude on Mother's part which
hardened me in my resolve to keep silent about all the
revelations made to me by Hermione. I felt pretty sure that,
in her present mood of wanting to get on with new neighbours like the Phillipses, Mother might well decide against
encouraging any friendship with Cora if she knew all
the gossip. She would feel uneasy about excluding her,
because she was usually very fair-minded, but she would
decide that it lay in our best interests as a family to go
along with local prejudice. That was the manner she was
already beginning to adopt, but she wasn't spelling it out
yet. She hoped I would be deflected by Hermione and her
friends and abandon Cora without any unpleasantness. I
thought that Father would have agreed with *me* about the

whole business, but then Father wasn't at home very much, and, when he was, local feuds weren't what he most wanted to hear about.

I did try to explain it all to Cora, though, difficult and potentially hurtful as that was. I thought that the only way of being fair to her was to tell her the difficulties I was having and why. One day we were wandering round the common in the sun. I was feeling a bit guilty because not only had Mother more or less put the graveyard out of bounds but she'd just about done the same with the common; Mrs. Phillips had heard some tales about nasty men lurking there and had advised everyone at the Mothers' Union to keep their children in their own gardens. "That's all right if you've got a garden the same as theirs but when you've just got a titchy little place like ours overrun with babies . . ." I'd said as I flounced out. Now, I was remembering her hurt face as she'd said, "I'm only thinking of you, darling." But then, I'd just banged the door and come straight to the common with Cora.

I said to Cora: "I must tell you something, Cora."

She looked at me and waited. She had the expression of someone steeling herself for a fatal blow, and it irritated me. It was time she realized how loyal I'd been in standing up for her. I was fed up with her looking as though I was going to let her down any minute when in fact I was putting myself through quite an amount of unpleasantness taking her part all the time. "Oh, for goodness' sake, Cora, don't be so pathetic! It makes me *want* to abandon you. I just want you to know there are gigantic snags cropping up for me because I'm friends with you, that's all."

"I'm sorry," she said, bleakly.

"Well, you must realize how it is. You've managed to put everyone in the village off you except for me. Every time I stick up for you it annoys people. They don't like me so much because they know I think you're all right."

"Well, I *am* all right," said Cora stubbornly. "They're wrong. Most of them are rich and smug and stupid."

I admired her defiance. She'd been alone for so long, faced rejection from all sides from the start, yet still she could stand up and fight back. I wasn't sure that I would have been able to. But another aspect of my relationship with her, which I certainly hadn't realized at first, was now beginning to dawn on me. It was that only now, for the first time, did she feel she had an ally; therefore the more she trusted me the worse would be the blow if I betrayed her. And who was to say how many more blows that abused personality could take? She was more vulnerable than ever because of me, because I had declared myself her friend. As it happened, I didn't want to betray her, but it would have been very difficult to opt out of the friendship now if, for some reason, I had wanted to.

"As a matter of fact you're probably right," I said. "But that doesn't make it any easier for me. Mummy wants me to be friends with people like Hermione Phillips. She wants us to fit in here and she wants people to like us. And the more I'm seen hanging around with you the less people are going to want me at their houses."

"Is it as bad as that?"

"Cora, you *know* it's as bad as that. The one good thing is that Mummy and Daddy don't know it yet. But when they do find out I've a feeling they might be as bad as the others and say I mustn't have anything to do with you."

"I thought they were fairer than that. You always said . . ."

"They are usually, particularly Daddy—but then he isn't here day after day. You can see what it's like for Mummy —all that pressure from neighbours. Not that I'm defending her but I just know she's hoping it'll fizzle out with you and that I'll get more and more friendly with Hermione and her cronies."

"Oh," said Cora in a flat voice. "Are you going to let it fizzle out? What do you think of Hermione, anyway?"

"I like her very much. I . . ."

"I don't know how you could. She's a snob! The whole family of Phillipses are a snooty lot. And her poetry—it's absolutely frightful. She doesn't understand nature at all."

"How do you know about her poetry?" I couldn't imagine Hermione ever showing Cora her notebooks.

"It's plastered all over the school magazine. That's how I know. Nobody can help knowing. She's the worst show-off I ever met."

"Still, if it's in the school magazine it must be good—the teachers must think it is."

Cora was subdued for a minute but then said firmly: "Well, I don't think it's any use at all. One day I'll show you my mum's poems and then you'll see what's good nature poetry and what isn't."

"Well, I'd like to see your mother's diaries, I must say. Why don't you bring them along with you next time?"

"Oh, I can't. I absolutely can't. Dad keeps them locked up and only lets me look at them when he's there. They're his most important treasures."

"Oh, I see. Perhaps he'd never let me see them."

"I think he might if you were at home with me . . . Will you come one day? It couldn't be all nice like at your house with proper cooked tea because Dad doesn't come in till later but . . ."

"I don't know, Cora. Let's leave it for a bit."

"Oh, I see. Tea at the Phillipses' is all right but it's a bit of a come-down to go to the Ravenwings'."

I was suddenly fed up with all her sneers and gibes. I snapped at her: "Oh! For Heaven's sake! I've had enough of you, Cora. You're so rude and unfair. Why should I be friends with you anyway? There's nothing in it for me." Then I turned away from her abruptly and stormed off at great speed.

My outburst brought her to a complete standstill for a moment but it wasn't long before I heard her flapping feet behind me. "Becky, Becky . . . wait, I'm sorry. I didn't mean it."

I ignored her until I was sure that my flash of temper had subsided. Then I slowed down and looked squarely in her face. She was so thin and distraught and that lank fringe was dangling in her eyes as usual. I brushed it aside so I could see her clearly and she could see me, and I held her face firmly in my hands, as I did sometimes with Jo when I really wanted him to listen to what I was going to say. "Oh, Cora! Let me be. Let me have friends if I want to. Let me see how it all works out. Don't plague me and taunt me and sneer at other people I like; that'll drive me away from you. If you're nice to me and fair to me I won't be nasty to you and leave you. Why should I?" Her sharp, dark eyes filled with tears and her head shifted and jerked uneasily between my hands. I let go of her. "I mean it, Cora. I can't stand you nagging and if you go on I'll have to stop being friends with you. But if you stop and if we can just have a bit of fun together instead of all this fuss all the time I'll like being with you."

"All right," she said. "I'm just scared the others'll put

you off me, but perhaps they won't. In any case I'll just have to risk it. I can see you aren't going to give them all up . . ."

"Of course I'm not. You wouldn't cut yourself off from everyone else by choice, would you? You'd like lots of friends yourself—I bet you would."

"I don't know; one'd do me. But, anyway, I can see you're different and I'll try to stop being jealous."

Afterwards I wondered if so much plain-speaking had been cruel. But it had seemed the only way of befriending Cora at all. I felt that much of my motive for keeping faith with her was simply pity for her predicament. At any rate it was very difficult to know what I would have thought of her if I'd met her under different circumstances. As it was, she'd attached herself to me from the outset like a mal-treated puppy and I had taken her on long before I realized the half of what was entailed.

The following Saturday afternoon I donned my second summer dress and set off, alone this time, for Stansfield House. I met a tall, pleasant-looking girl at the gate; she was obviously a fellow-guest and we introduced ourselves. Her name was Barbara Foster and she had reddish wavy hair and quite a lot of freckles. She was very easy to get on with but not very interesting; I didn't feel half-scared of her as I had at first of Hermione, with her blonde beauty and intense manner. I thought that Mother would have thought Barbara a perfect companion for me, with her fresh complexion, open smile, and friendly ways. In a way I was glad that she wasn't going to be a challenge, one was enough, but I knew from the outset that I'd never value her friendship as much as Hermione's.

"I hear you're going to be in our class at school," said Barbara. "Mummy said Mrs. Phillips thought so. It's Miss

Dingwall's class *we're* going into. Have you been told whose form you're to be in?"

"I think Mummy's got a letter from the headmistress somewhere but it's been mislaid during all the chaos of house-moving. That name rings a bell, though."

"It'll be nice if you *are* in with us. You must sit with our gang. We usually bag desks next to each other—two side by side and one behind. It'll be nice to be a foursome so that the one behind doesn't feel out of it."

I thought it was very kind of her to include me so readily and wondered if Hermione and Susan Spenser, whom I had yet to meet, would agree. "I'd love that. But perhaps Hermione and Susan . . ."

"Oh, Hermione can be a bit moody sometimes but she doesn't mean anything by it. We just ignore it. She's a poetic type, you know. I'm sure Susan'll take to you just like that. She can be a bit mad and giggly; she's the one that gets us into trouble now and then. But she's great fun, a real scream . . . and ever so good at art."

Susan and Hermione were waiting for us by the front door. They were sitting on the back bumper of a big white car, scraping the dusty gravel with their feet and looking a bit bored with each other. Susan leapt up and ran over when she saw us and Barbara introduced us. Susan dropped into an elaborate curtsey and Barbara gave her a poke. "Don't act the goat, Susan. Give Rebecca a chance."

"Oh, call me Becky," I said. "Rebecca's just for people I don't know very well."

They both said they liked Becky better and then Barbara nudged Susan and pointed across at Hermione, who hadn't moved and wasn't taking any notice of us. "What's up with her?"

"Goodness knows! She's been like that since I arrived. Another poem brewing probably!"

"Baggy not interrupt," said Barbara.

"Nor me," said Susan quickly. "That leaves you, Becky. Probably best if you speak to her first anyway. She's bound to be nice as you're new."

"Isn't she always nice?"

"We think she's a bit spoiled," said Barbara. "But we don't really mind because she's super most of the time."

Susan said: "It's just that she writes poetry and sometimes she gets a bit superior about it—at least that's what we think, don't we, Barb? Bit rude, though, sticking herself in a poetic trance your first visit." She adopted an exaggerated pose, pretending to be lost in elevated thought, and then burst out giggling.

I felt cross on Hermione's behalf. "Oh, I've been before. I don't mind going up and speaking to her first," I said. "Actually, I write poems myself, and Hermione and I have read quite a lot of each other's work." I left them looking a bit pink-faced and walked over to Hermione. I sat down beside her on the bumper. "Hello, Hermione. It's another super day, isn't it?"

"Mmm? . . . Oh, hello," she said as if she hadn't realized till then that Barbara and I had arrived. I thought that was a bit affected and silly, as she must have heard us and she must have been aware of Susan running over to greet us. But she carried it all off with such poise and style that I was still impressed. I could never have attempted a similar display. I was too ordinary; I should have looked ridiculous if I'd tried to seem vague or lost in a reverie. "Oh, hello, Becky," she said mistily. "It is a super day, you're right. I've been in Paradise all morning working on a new poem and I can hardly clear my mind of it."

"It seems a pity to try," I said. "Would you like the three of us to have a walk round the garden and leave you alone for a bit?"

"Oh no. That wouldn't do at all. Mummy'd be awfully cross and say it was the height of bad manners." She sighed and rose dutifully from the bumper. "No—I'm all right now. I want to come with you. It's just difficult sometimes to switch moods, isn't it? You'll know that yourself . . ."

"Oh, yes, I know exactly what you mean," I said, delighted to be considered a soul-mate. We went over and joined the others. They were relieved to find Hermione coaxed out of her poetical mood so quickly.

"I didn't mean to be rude about poetry," said Susan later, as we wandered across to the paddock to see the horses. Barbara and Hermione were some distance ahead and couldn't hear us. "It's just that it's so embarrassing when Hermione turns herself off like that. I get all unnerved and giggly and that just makes her cross. Barb's awfully good with her, actually—just carries on as usual right through all the ups and downs."

"Barbara says you're artistic yourself," I said.

"Well, I suppose so," she said modestly. "I'm not much good at anything else, anyway. Mummy and Daddy both paint, so it's in the family. Hermione and Barb are both brainy though—you probably don't know that. Hermione was top in English last term and Barb got ninety-eight per cent in the arithmetic exam. Are you frightfully clever too? It'd be nice to have someone in our gang who was just ordinary like me."

"I think I'm ordinary," I said. "If I'm good at anything it's English. But I don't see how I could be as good as Hermione."

"No, I suppose she is rather special," Susan agreed, and

envious feelings stirred inside me. I wanted to be as good as Hermione.

This time, it turned out that Mr. and Mrs. Phillips were away for the afternoon and there was absolutely no sign of the boys. When we went in for tea we found the kitchen table laid for the four of us. It looked like a party table with flowery paper napkins and straws sticking up out of our tumblers and a white-iced cake and trifle. "Oh goody," said Hermione. "Horti's made us our tea. I'll go and tell her we're ready."

"Wait till you see Horti," said Susan mischievously when Hermione was out of the room.

"Why?" I asked. "What's wrong with her?"

"Ooh, là, là!" said Susan. "Nothing's wrong, exactly. She's just terribly French. She's the *au pair*, you know. Very fancy set-up they have here."

Hermione came back and poured out orange juice and handed round egg sandwiches. They seemed to have some sort of herb flavouring, and at first I found it very off-putting. But by the time I'd reached my third I was enjoying the new taste. Then the door opened and in came Horti; she stepped neatly across to the oven and took out a plate of sausage rolls. She was small and black-haired with brown skin and dark eyes. She was wearing a scarlet silk scarf over her hair, a scarlet blouse and black skirt, stockings and shoes. There was a broad shiny belt around her waist with a big gold buckle. She balanced the plate aloft on one hand like a waitress and tripped elegantly across to the table. "Hello, girls," she said and smiled warmly at all of us. She put the plate down in the middle of the table. "Tuck in. Right?"

Hermione said: "Right! Very good! Horti, you must meet Becky—she's the one I've been talking about, the one who writes poetry."

Horti stepped smartly round the table and shook my hand. "How do you do, Becky?" she said. "It's nice to see you here. It's a lovely house, isn't it? And a lovely family. I love it here. Now, Hermione, *chérie*, if you want something else come and get me. I'm in my room." She turned, and her black skirt swirled round with her. Then off she went, darting us a last bright smile as she went out.

Susan could scarcely wait for the door to close before giggling and spluttering into her orange juice and mimicking Horti to a tee. "'Ello, 'ello! Ooh, 'Ermione, *chérie*! Come eef you need me." She burst into streams of mock-French, throwing her arms in the air and flashing her eyes in all directions.

I thought Hermione would be angry, but she smiled indulgently across at Susan and waited for her to stop. "Try not to be a complete ass, Sue," she said at last. Then she turned to me and said: "Horti's super, actually. Her real name's Hortense, you know. She's from Normandy. She's been with us eighteen months now. Mummy says she's pure gold."

"Go on," said Susan, giggling. "Tell Becky how she's teaching you French . . ."

"So she is," said Hermione. "What's wrong with that?"

Firmly and quickly Barbara said: "Nothing."

I was thinking all the time that I'd seen Horti before, and suddenly I remembered. "I've seen her before," I exclaimed. "—On the common."

"The common!" said Hermione.

"Yes. She was with your big brother."

When I saw Hermione's expression I wished I'd kept my mouth shut. Even Susan managed to keep silent, though bursting with glee.

"Are you sure?"

"Well—yes. Just walking they were . . ."

"But Mummy won't hear of any of us going to the common. Which brother, anyway?"

"The biggest one—Hector, is it?"

"Hector and Horti!"

"Just walking . . ." I muttered.

"Oh, come on, Hermione," said Barbara. "Hector's over twenty now."

Hermione looked down at her plate. "Oh, it's not that," she mumbled. "It's just that she never said . . . I don't expect she means half she says to me. I bet she's no intention of having me to stay when she goes back. And she knows Mummy thinks people who loiter around on the common are—common."

We all laughed uproariously at her little joke, but Hermione didn't. I hoped she wouldn't mention to her parents that I had been on the common, let alone Horti. "I'm terribly sorry," I said nervously. "I wish I hadn't said."

She sighed deeply. I thought she was going to cry, but suddenly she smiled at me and said: "Don't be silly, Becky. I'm being daft. It's just that I've always thought Horti was marvellous. And I thought she considered me an equal and told me everything. But of course she doesn't. Not surprising really."

Susan said: "I do think you're being brave, Hermione. I'm sorry I teased you so much earlier on. It's rotten finding out that someone hasn't been honest."

"Yes," agreed Barbara, "—that awful let-down feeling."

"Oh, she's not such a rat, really," said Hermione. "I'm always thinking I'm more important than I really am."

We all protested and consoled her. We each said why we thought she *was* important. And, to my relief, I found that the incident had actually pulled me right into the heart of the group where, at first, I thought I'd ruined my chances with my unguarded chatter.

Towards the end of the meal Barbara returned to the subject of school. "I thought it'd be nice if Becky sat with us next term. What do you think?" she asked the others.

"Oh, certainly," said Hermione. "I'll sit next to her, shall I, as we've got so much in common with our poetry?"

Barbara and Susan were full of approval of the plan and I felt extremely happy. Okington was going to be wonderful. Here I was with three special friends already, one of a gang . . . Dimly a vision of Cora flitted through my mind, a tiny shadow so swiftly banished as scarcely to register. My friendship with Cora would just have to be fitted in behind everything else. Hermione and the others came first. I could not imagine ever choosing Cora's company in preference to theirs.

Chapter 6 ❧ The Birthday Party

THE NEXT WEEK, THE LAST OF THE HOLIDAYS, INCLUDED MY birthday. I'd thought it would have to be a very quiet affair this year, with the house move and no friends in the area to ask to a party. But now it seemed there could be a party after all and Mother was almost insistent that there should be. I personally thought it would seem a bit forward to ask such new acquaintances to celebrate my birthday with me. "They'll think they've got to bring a present. It's a bit much when they hardly know me."

"Rubbish! All you girls like parties. You can have it in the garden. It'll be lovely."

"But still—the present business . . ."

"It's not going to bother the Phillipses buying you a little present."

"The others, though. Maybe they have to spend their own pocket-money on things like that."

"Well, all right. How about asking them to come and only telling them it's your birthday when they arrive?"

That seemed a good idea. It would also mean I didn't need to worry about what to wear. I still felt that Mother was rushing things a bit—it might have been more appropriate for Susan and Barbara to have had me to their homes first—but I assumed she knew she was doing the right thing. In the event, she rang all the mothers herself and I could hear her explaining that it was my birthday and she wanted me to have a little party as usual. I heard her saying to Mrs. Spenser: "It's her birthday, actually, but she's shy of telling the others so we're keeping it a secret . . . But it seems a shame for the poor little soul not to celebrate in some way . . . And perhaps you'd like to pop in yourself towards the end, just for a cup of tea—or something a bit stronger! It'd be so nice to meet you . . ." Then I realized that at least half the point of the party was that Mother and Father should meet the parents. I wasn't yet used to considering their problems very deeply. But, of course, this would be the perfect opportunity for them to make the acquaintance of the Spensers and the Fosters at the same time as keeping things ticking over with the Phillipses.

My birthday was on Thursday but the party was arranged for the following Saturday afternoon. The new school term was to start on the Tuesday of the next week. My actual birthday was fairly uneventful except for the arrival of a pleasing number of cards from old school friends who said they were missing me. I felt a little faithless, as I'd been concentrating so hard on making new friends that I'd scarcely given the old ones a thought. I think it was this feeling of disloyalty which led me to do a rather foolish thing in the afternoon.

I'd been sent a ten shilling note by a great-aunt and had gone down to Copcutt's to spend some of it on sweets. I was wandering slowly home with a packet of peanuts and some peardrops when I met Cora. I jumped guiltily because I hadn't seen her for a day or two and expected an instant tirade of abuse. But it didn't come. She smiled and said: "Becky! It's nice to see you. Are you free for a bit? Shall we go for a walk?" I was grateful to her for being so affable and agreed to spend the afternoon with her. After we'd told Mother we were going for a walk we set off together, sharing the sweets and talking easily and happily. I told her it was my birthday and she sang "Happy Birthday" in clear, true tones which took me utterly by surprise.

"You've got a lovely voice, Cora."

"That's about the only thing I inherited from my mum," she said.

"You don't look as if you could sing. I'd never thought of you as musical, somehow. Can you play any instruments?"

"A bit. Can you?"

I told her about my piano lessons. I had taken the fourth grade exam shortly before leaving Birmingham and had just heard I'd gained a distinction, so I was feeling rather proud of myself. I thought Cora looked impressed and forgot to ask any further details about her own music. She was in her usual mood of just simply asking and listening, not divulging much about herself. As we made our way up the lane past the church she stopped suddenly and said: "Becky, come in again. You haven't been in for ages."

"Mummy says I'm not to . . . I've promised. She says people don't like children jumping over the graves, dishonouring their dead."

"You know I'd never do that." She looked hurt. "I've a perfect right to go in when it's my own mother that's buried here. If you don't mind my saying so, your mother isn't always absolutely right. You know perfectly well we've never misbehaved here."

She was right, of course. "But I'm still a bit scared, Cora," I admitted. "I know it sounds daft to you when you're so used to the place, but I suddenly get the idea that a ghost might appear or something. It's so quiet and spooky."

"Oh, Becky! Don't be silly! Just look in over the gate. It's the most beautiful garden you've ever seen, isn't it?" Certainly the graveyard did seem peaceful and ageless with the sun beating down on the flowering shrubs and the yew trees casting their cool dark shadows over the grass and the birds whistling all at once. "Doesn't Dad keep it nice?" said Cora proudly.

"It's lovely," I said. "All right. I'll come."

"Here, hold my hand," she said and grasped me securely. "Don't be frightened." She led me through the gate. "I won't dance or talk strangely. Don't worry. Trust me." She led me along the little pathway beside the church and we didn't trample over any of the grassy mounds I'd so dreaded before. At the back of the church we came upon her mother's grave again. "I just wanted you to see her roses," said Cora. "Aren't they beautiful? I'm going to pick you some for your birthday . . ."

"Oh, you mustn't do that, Cora," I gasped.

"Don't be silly. Why not? She'd want you to have some."

I could feel myself beginning to panic again. The idea of gathering a dead woman's roses was making my skin tighten all over. "Don't touch them, Cora," I said in a clipped voice. "Not for me. I don't really want them."

She looked disappointed. "Becky, don't worry," she said gently. "I know what you're thinking and, if that's how you feel, of course I won't pick any. But they're just flowers, you know—it makes no difference where they're growing or why they were planted here." Her voice was firm and even. Again I was aware of the inner confidence and strength which seemed to possess her whenever she visited this familar territory.

"It's funny how you change in here, Cora," I said. "You're much surer of yourself. You should be like this all the time. In here I really feel you're my equal and you help me not to be frightened, but when we're outside I always feel in charge of you somehow."

"Nobody ever bothers me in here," said Cora. "I feel safe here. But there isn't anywhere else I feel safe."

"Not even at home?"

"Well, yes. At home, sometimes, if Dad's there. But often he's not, and I get lonely."

"Why don't you tell him? Perhaps he'd come home earlier."

"He's lonely too."

Rather than sink into gloom contemplating the Raven-wings' sad situation I suggested a walk on the common, and we soon recovered our earlier good spirits. Cora picked me a bunch of wild flowers; she spotted them in hollows and crannies where I would never have seen them myself. Then she sang "Happy Birthday" again, and again I was struck by the clarity of her voice and said so. She seemed, this time, to retain her graveyard vitality for quite a while after we left and I silently noted her bright face and light movements. The jerking and flapping mannerisms didn't return till we were on our way home. It was then that I made my foolhardy move. We'd had such a pleasant afternoon and Cora had been such cheerful company that, without thought, I opened my mouth and said: "I'm having a party on Saturday, Cora. Would you like to come?"

She stopped dead, right in the middle of the pavement,

and clasped her hands together in great excitement. "Oh, Becky! How super! Nobody's ever asked me to a party before."

At once I knew the invitation was a huge mistake. But it was too late. It would have been cruel to retract it. All the time that I was explaining who the other guests would be and when to come and what to wear I knew that I shouldn't have asked her.

At home Mother said non-committally: "Oh, you've asked Cora, have you? Was that wise? It'll make an odd number. Will she fit in with the others?"

"Oh, yes," I said. "It'll be all right. They're in the same form at school, after all." Mother just nodded. She still had no real reason to suspect that Cora's presence might be disastrous. She'd still heard none of the gossip that I'd heard.

"I've asked Mrs. Briggs to come and give me a hand on Saturday afternoon," she said. "She can put the finishing touches to the food and that'll leave Daddy and me free to help organize games and keep the boys from under your feet."

"Mrs. Briggs!" I said horrified. "Oh, we don't want her, Mummy. She's so managing. She'll take over the whole thing. Can't we keep it just family? I don't even like her." The idea of Cora and the other three sitting together round the one tea-table was difficult enough to contemplate, but with Mrs. Briggs as hostess . . . that *must* be prevented. Goodness only knew what sort of outburst might result.

"Becky! Don't be silly! It'll be ideal to have someone handling the kitchen end of things. Anyway, I've asked her —it's all arranged."

There was nothing I could do. I lay awake most of Thursday night battling to find a solution but the only way out seemed to involve cancelling Cora's invitation and I couldn't bring myself to be so mean—not after witnessing her immense pleasure at being included for once. By the time Friday dawned I had decided to put every effort into making the party a success despite all my misgivings. I spent the day helping Mother make little cakes and trifle, blow up balloons and set up a treasure-hunt in the garden. We even erected a table under the trees so that we could have our tea outside and I felt that that would largely eliminate the danger of unpleasantness from Mrs. Briggs. She could glower at Cora and mutter all the calumnies she liked from the kitchen window; nobody would hear or notice her.

But when I came to in my bed on Saturday morning all my hopes were dashed. I could hear the steady drum of heavy rain against the roof and window-panes and knew at once that we were all going to be confined for the afternoon in our little front room. I tore downstairs in my pyjamas. Father was finishing his breakfast and reading the paper and Mother was putting out cereal and making toast for me and the boys. "Look at the rain!" I said. "Let's cancel it. It'll be hopeless. Let's just scrap it."

"For Heaven's sake, Becky!" said Father. "What's all this about? We'll have the party inside. It's not that difficult."

"Oh, it is, Daddy. It'll be hopeless," I said, bursting into tears. "It's not what we'd planned at all, is it, Mummy?"

Mother looked astonished and cross at the fuss I was making. "Pull yourself together, Becky. Of course it's disappointing but we can't just cancel because of a bit of rain. Everybody would think we were mad!"

"Well, we can't have the treasure-hunt now, can we? That's what people like best. That's all spoiled. All the clues'll be sodden out there," I said desperately. I already knew I wasn't going to win.

"Jo and I will set up a new treasure-hunt indoors," said Father in an effort to appease me. "Now go upstairs and get your clothes on. Your mother'll need your help getting things tidied up this morning."

I went heavily back upstairs. There seemed no way in which the afternoon could be anything but calamitous.

Mrs. Briggs arrived first. She came at about two-thirty to help with sandwiches and setting the table. When the doorbell rang my heart started pounding in my chest. It must be Cora an hour early! But when I opened the door it was Mrs. Briggs, her face all red and wet, a plastic rain-hat tied tightly over her head and a soaking black rain-cape buttoned up under the chin. As she stepped in she filled the hall with the nasty smell of not-very-fresh wet clothes. "That's better," she panted as she struggled out of the cape and hung it over the end of the banisters. She untied the plastic hat, shook out her grizzled hair and patted it into some sort of style. I fancied the smell in the hall thickened. In horror I stared at the flowery frilly dress she was wearing. "Admiring my dress?" she asked, pirouetting clumsily around and flouncing out the skirt which had been crushed by her rain-cape. "No good going to a party and not wearing your glad rags, is it, dear? How do I look?"

"Nice," I mumbled. She looked like one of the ugly sisters dressed up for the ball. "I'll tell Mummy you're here."

"Just a minute," she said, fumbling around in the baggy hold-all she always carried. "Let me get out me fancy apron. And there's a little something here for you."

Mother came out of the kitchen at that moment. "Mrs. Briggs! Not a present!" she said in tones of mock crossness. "What did I say? Nobody's supposed to know it's a *birth-day* party!"

"What *I* say," said Mrs. Briggs, pulling out a package and handing it to me, "is that a birthday's a birthday—secret or not. And a birthday means presents. Isn't that right, dear?" She gave me a grotesque wink.

I pulled off the wrapping paper, wondering what on earth I was going to find and how I would be able to look grateful. Mother said: "You're very wicked, Mrs. Briggs; you shouldn't have bothered. Isn't it kind of Mrs. Briggs, darling?" Inside the outer wrapping was a twist of white tissue paper and, as I opened that, a little shiny bracelet dropped on to the floor. It had a single charm on it and, when I bent to pick it up, I saw it was a horrid little hob-goblin figure, with an ugly gaping mouth, who seemed to be hopping round on one leg, the other bent up in front of him and held at the ankle. I was speechless—but Mother and Mrs. Briggs were not. "Let me see, dear," said Mother "How fascinating! I haven't seen anything like this, Mrs. Briggs."

"No. Unusual, isn't it?" said Mrs. Briggs smugly. "I thought you'd like it. Copcutt's have got a whole batch in. They're novelty charm bracelets. That's a special good-luck goblin to start you off . . . no, don't wrap it up again, dear. Wear it for your party."

"Shouldn't I keep it safe?" I appealed to Mother, hoping she would understand how much I wanted to put the thing out of sight.

She did understand but chose to ignore me. "No, no, dear. Of course you must wear it today. What a lovely idea. Here . . . I'll do it up for you. Now, what about changing into a dress . . .?"

"I thought I wasn't dressing up. I thought everyone was coming in ordinary clothes."

"Well, now we're obviously not going to be outside, I expect the others will put nice dresses on."

"Of course they will," seconded Mrs. Briggs. "Go on, dear. You slip on something pretty. You won't feel a birthday girl if you don't make an effort—And I won't let you keep on your new bracelet!"

I was beginning to think it didn't much matter what I wore or what other changes of plan Mrs. Briggs managed to engineer, the whole afternoon was doomed in any case. As I plodded numbly upstairs I heard Mother saying: "She's terribly disappointed about the weather, I'm afraid. Do excuse her. I expect she'll cheer up soon."

"Oh, don't apologize, dear," said Mrs. Briggs. "I'm used to kids, remember."

I glanced back at her; she was pulling a lurid shiny apron over her head—another "glad rag".

At half-past three on the dot the doorbell rang again and I went to open it. By this time the boys had been taken next door to be out of the way and I'd put on my only party dress, which Mother had always assured me was not only very pretty but also a "good garment". It was broderie anglaise, with narrow, crimson, velvet ribbon threaded through at the neck, waist and hem. I'd also put on my white angora bolero to please Mother. These tiny jackets were very much the fashion amongst girls at the time—we nearly all had one. I hated mine; it had been knitted by my grandmother and the wool was rather thick and matted where it should have been like fluffy down round my shoulders. Barbara and Susan were standing in a huddle on the doorstep, giggling and chattering and holding brightly wrapped packages above their heads to keep the rain off their hair. They looked excited and pretty and for a second my spirits soared as they jumped inside, saying: "Happy birthday, Becky! I knew you'd be in a party dress!"

"Have a present!"

"I've only put a frock on because Mummy insisted," I said. "You're not supposed to know it's a birthday party. You shouldn't have brought presents!"

Mother came through from the kitchen. She looked cheerful and fresh in a crisp cotton dress. "Hello, girls . . . now I specifically said . . . Becky, aren't they naughty? . . . Well, you must look now, dear. What kind new friends . . .!"

Susan had brought me a new pencil case and Barbara had brought chocolates. We all had one at once while they took their coats off and shambled hesitantly into the front room, where Father was fiddling with the record player. "Snap!" said Susan, pointing at my bolero; she was wearing one too, over a silky orange dress with a huge sash. Barbara was wearing a sensible plain navy dress with white buttons and she'd put a white band in her hair. I could see Mother thought them a very nice pair of girls, just the sort I should be mixing with. And Father looked just as pleased as he rose to greet them. I left him putting them at their ease to open the door for Hermione, who arrived at that moment. As she came in I spotted Cora approaching the gate, but instead of holding the door open for her I slammed it quickly. I wanted just a few seconds with Hermione before Cora's presence jinxed everything. Hermione's father had delivered her at the door in the big white car and she was hardly wet at all. She was wearing a green velvet cape with a fur collar, and underneath she had on a pink dress trimmed with lace, and she had brought soft pink shoes to change into. She gave me a present to open while she changed her shoes; it was a collection of poems by Walter de la Mare.

I said: "Hermione! That's my best present of all!"

Then Mother was bustling into the hall and sweeping

her off into the front room as the doorbell rang again for Cora, the last and fatal guest! My heart was black with treachery as I contemplated not opening the door. I wished she'd be suddenly sick and have to go; I wished I could just stick my head round the door and hiss: "Buzz off!" I wished I'd never in my life had anything to do with her. But, with profound reluctance, I opened the door and looked wanly out at her.

"Becky!" she said smiling. "Happy birthday!" She held out a damp little parcel. ". . . Can I come in?" A big shiver ran right through her. She was drenched and cold.

"Oh, come on in, Cora," I said. I was relieved that the actual sight of her brought me back to reality. How could such a drab, wet little creature provoke anything but pity? She was so limp and insignificant the others would hardly notice her. She could just sit by the fire and dry out while the rest of us went ahead with the fun and games.

"I thought nobody was dressing up, Becky," she said, worried when she stepped round the door and saw my party dress.

"Change of plan—because of the weather." I said. "Don't worry. It doesn't matter at all."

"Oh, I wish you'd said . . ." She looked upset as she took off her macintosh and stood there in the usual navy tee-shirt and shorts, the rain gathering in droplets along the ends of her fringe. She struggled out of her wellingtons and pulled on the black gym shoes she'd brought for inside. "I have got a frock, you know."

"I'm sorry, Cora. You'll be fine. Come on; the others are here already. Come and get warm." I wanted to get on with the moment of confrontation. Sounds of music and mirth were coming from the front room. I wanted everyone to know the worst as soon as possible.

As I pushed the front room door open I caught sight of Father grinning, his hand hovering over the gramophone pick-up. Susan and Barbara were thumping up and down to the music and Hermione was taking rather more elegant skips and jumps in a corner; Mother was looking on from an arm-chair, smiling gently. Cora and I stepped in as Father lifted the pick-up. The music stopped. Susan, Barbara and Hermione crashed to the floor in a giggling heap. "Still not too old for musical bumps!" said Father to me. "Now. Who's this? Do we all know each other?"

One by one the others sat up and stopped laughing. "Cora!" said Mother. "My dear, you're soaked! Come and sit by the fire with me and get dry. Becky, run and get a towel, love."

So I left the room and didn't see the immediate effect of Cora's entrance. I didn't see if there were any nudges, faces pulled, whisperings . . . or if Father sensed a sudden chill. By the time I came back with the towel Cora was huddled at Mother's feet and the others were watching Susan unwrap a prize she'd won for the musical bumps. The next hour passed pleasantly enough, I thought. I was glad Father had worked out a non-stop programme of games. I had protested earlier in the day that we were all getting rather old for organized games, but now they provided the perfect excuse for the others to ignore Cora totally without it appearing the least obvious. We all soberly and intently applied ourselves to games which would normally have given rise to much roistering about. By the time it was a quarter to five and Mother excused herself to put the finishing touches to tea I was almost enjoying myself.

Mother reappeared in a few moments and asked us all to go through to the dining-room. The afternoon was overcast and dark and when we went in I was surprised to find that the curtains had been drawn and the room was lit with candles. The girls were all very delighted with the effect; Father helped them into their chairs and they started to pull crackers and put on paper hats. Only I, at first, noticed Mrs. Briggs lurking in a dark corner, her red face glistening under a pointed paper hat. I watched her as Cora shuffled in, last in the line. Her eyes bulged like marbles, her face loomed purple in the flickering light. She made an explosive sound like a stifled sneeze. Then I watched Cora, waited for her to spot Mrs. Briggs in the shadows. When she did, she choked on a sausage-roll and Father had to thump her on the back rather hard to dislodge the crumbs. Mrs. Briggs enjoyed that. I thought she'd probably like to be in Father's place, hammering away at poor Cora's bony little spine. The meal progressed; the food was delicious; Mother and Mrs. Briggs made sure our plates were never empty. It wasn't obvious that Mrs. Briggs never offered anything to Cora. I was at one end of the table and Hermione and Barbara were on either side of me; Father sat down at the other end and acted the clown, to Susan's delight; even Cora couldn't help laughing at him. At the end Mother brought in my birthday cake with its candles and I blew them out while the girls sang "Happy Birthday." Cora's voice rose sweet and clear with the others. Everyone wanted the candles lit a second time, so we repeated the procedure and afterwards Mother said: "What a beautiful voice you've got, Cora." And Cora, warmed through, smiled like a little pixy under her dark cap of hair.

Father said: "Bet you're full of secrets, Cora, eh?" I could see he was rather captivated by her shy, hesitant manner. And certainly he was favouring her now as he sensed that, for some reason, she was odd one out. Perhaps it even pleased him to thwart Mrs. Briggs, whose outburst against Cora he could not have forgotten. When we'd eaten all we could he swept Cora out of the dining-room right under her nose, saying: "A rare blackbird we've got here, don't you think, Mrs. Briggs?"

After tea Mother organized us in the front room again. She decided we should have a Beetle drive while we digested our food and soon we were all seated round the card-table, heads lowered, dice rattling. We had three or four games, and Cora won most of them and was presented with a prize at the end, which nobody seemed to resent. After this, things became less orderly. Mother and Father decided that we could entertain ourselves for the time remaining and they retired to the kitchen to have a cup of tea with Mrs. Briggs. Joseph and Dorian were delivered back from next door and came bursting in to see what they'd missed. They loaded themselves up with chocolate biscuits from the dining table and, after initial shyness, started to show off to the girls.

I myself eventually suggested a game of hide-and-seek all over the house. I wasn't sure that Mother and Father would approve, so I insisted that everyone keep very quiet—no yelling, shouting or thundering up and down stairs. It turned out to be rather exciting as we all crept stealthily about in the gathering gloom; Mother and Father hadn't switched on the upstairs lights yet as they hadn't been expecting us to leave the front room. After a while I became aware that nobody was looking for Cora any more and that she'd been hidden for ages. When it was my turn to seek I searched high and low for her but couldn't find her and decided not to hold the game up on her account. I never mentioned her to the others, nor did I suggest that they try to find her. As a matter of fact I thought that, as things had gone so well, it didn't really matter if she was abandoned in some dusty corner for the last half hour or so. I could always find her when everyone else had gone home, and make some sort of amends.

We had just finished a round of the game and were all laughing and flopping about in the front room when the kitchen door opened, and Mrs. Briggs came out and headed for the stairs.

"That's Mrs. Briggs going upstairs for something," I said. "Better not muck around up there for a bit with her on the prowl. Let's have another game of Beetle or something."

We began to organize ourselves desultorily when suddenly appalling screams from upstairs filled the house. My heart leapt. I rushed into the hall. Mother and Father burst out of the kitchen. Mrs. Briggs, panting and shouting, rushed wildly down the stairs with Dory in her arms.

"She's killing him! She's killing him!" she shrieked as Mother seized him and he burst into screams of fright. "First her mother, then my baby, then the Spenser baby—now yours! I'll get her, the little devil . . . !" She turned, her eyes glaring madly, and made for the stairs again. Father grabbed her. It took all his strength to hold her. Over his shoulder he ordered me and the others back into the front room. As I closed the door behind us I saw him hauling Mrs. Briggs into the kitchen and soon afterwards we heard his footsteps on the stairs. He was going up for Cora.

Susan was sobbing on the settee and Barbara was comforting her. Hermione sat motionless and white on the floor. After a while, when she started chewing her fingers, I dared to approach her and speak.

"I'm sorry. I don't know what on earth's happened . . ."

She hissed: "Didn't I tell you? I warned you. I wasn't supposed to but I did. I told you all about her. But you still invited her. You must be mad!"

"I didn't realize . . . I didn't mean . . ."

"It's too late now. Look at Susan. What effect do you think it's had on her?"

I crawled across the carpet and knelt before Susan, looking up into her trembling, wet face. She and Barbara had heard nothing of what Hermione had said. "Susan, I'm sorry. I'm sorry."

"It's not your fault," said Susan bravely, wiping her face. "You couldn't have known about her and what she did to my little brother."

"Oh yes she could," said Hermione with icy clarity. ". . . I told her."

"But I didn't understand," I pleaded as I saw shock hit the faces of the other two. "Forgive me. I can see it all now. I won't speak to her again. Not ever." I burst into tears myself. "Don't chuck me out because of this . . . *Please* don't."

It was Barbara, sensible Barbara, who made the decision. "It's O.K., Becky. Don't fret," she said. "Even if Hermione told you the facts I can see how hard it would be for a newcomer to understand. I suppose it was even nice of you to try and be friends with Cora—but it can't be done, you see . . ."

"Oh, I can see that now. Honestly I can. I shan't try again."

"Well, *I* think that's good enough," said Barbara. "What about you?" She looked at Susan and Hermione.

Susan sniffed in a determined and final way and stuffed her hanky up the little fluffy sleeve of her bolero. She sighed. "All right," she said. "Let's forget it. It's been a super party apart from this bit. And I do want you to be our friend at school. But no more Cora. Please, no more . . ."

"There won't be. I promise," I interrupted.

Hermione was silent. We all waited for her to speak, but she was still staring dumbly down at the carpet when the door opened and Cora slipped in. She made for the nearest corner and slid to the floor. There she sat, hugging her knees, head lowered, until the first parents arrived. That's how we were, silent and visibly shaken, when Mother and Father walked in with the Spensers. Susan rushed out for her coat and was buttoned into it in seconds. There was just time enough for her parents to notice the abject Cora. Then they turned and made for the front door with Susan before Father could so much as suggest sherry. The Phillipses and Fosters came and went in much the same way. Then Mr. Ravenwing arrived for Cora. I opened the door but didn't ask him in and Mother and Father didn't appear at all. He was all muffled up in a coat and scarf, and I could hardly make out his words as he asked for Cora. She looked surprised to see him but she scuttled out without a word. That was the end of my party.

I stood in the hall for a moment before daring to go into the kitchen. I couldn't imagine what would be going on in there but I could hear Mrs. Briggs, only partially calmed, by the sound of it, talking on and on and on . . . At last I opened the door and went in. Jo and Dory were playing on the floor with their cars; they were subdued but not unduly upset. Mother and Father and Mrs. Briggs were in a tight group around the table, leaning over their cups and talking keenly.

Mother was saying: "It's an *awful* tale, Mrs. Briggs! I wish I'd known before. I'd never have had the child in the house."

"Mental, she is," muttered Mrs. Briggs. "Or worse . . ."

"Now, now, Mrs. Briggs . . ." said Father.

"You mark my words, a child of the devil."

"I can't accept that . . ."

"Well . . . but, Edwin . . ." began Mother.

"Well but nothing," said Father. "Disturbed she may be. The child's had a very disturbing life. But 'child of the devil' —no—that I won't have. I'm not saying include her in everything, or even anything, come to that. But I won't be party to malicious slander."

"After what she nearly did to your own son?" gasped Mrs. Briggs. "Damn near suffocated him . . ."

"What *did* Cora do?" I asked in a small, shocked voice.

They all turned on me. They hadn't heard me open the door. Mother stretched out an arm. "Oh, Becky, sweetheart. What an awful end to your party and after it had all gone so beautifully too."

I went and stood beside her at the table and she put her arm round my waist. "What did Cora do?" I asked again.

"Not very much when it comes down to brass tacks," said Father eyeing Mrs. Briggs sharply and standing up. "She hid in the airing-cupboard when you were playing hide-and-seek. She took Dory in with her and closed the door. Mrs. Briggs went up for clean tea-towels, opened the door, and there they were, huddled up asleep like two dormice. Too hot, you see . . ."

"She could have killed him," said Mrs. Briggs. "That's what she nearly . . ."

"In that case she'd have killed herself too," said Father briskly. "Now we can't have any more of this. It was your mistake, Mrs. Briggs . . . and an understandable one in view of the things you've told us. But . . ."

"Surely Cora didn't want to kill Dory!" I said.

"Of course not," said Mother gently. "The airing-cupboard's not airtight anyway. And if she'd wanted to do anything cruel she wouldn't have got in there beside him. She was just hiding. But Mrs. Briggs got an awful fright when she opened the door and they were both squashed up in there with their eyes shut. For a second she thought they were dead."

Mrs. Briggs was mumbling under her breath throughout this explanation and at the end of it she said to me: "She's a bad child, that Cora. I've told you that before. None of the other children have anything to do with her. None of the other parents will have her to their homes. You shouldn't have asked her to your party. You know she's bad, don't you?" Her bulging eyes leered at me. I wondered if she knew I'd been told the local tales about Cora or if she was guessing.

Mother said quickly: "Oh, Becky couldn't know anything about what you've told us, Mrs. Briggs, and I think it best that she doesn't."

"Quite," said Father. "Come on, Becky, you come with me and we'll start a spot of tidying up."

But Mrs. Briggs kept on glaring at me and I found it hard to break away from her basilisk stare. She knew I knew.

Mother had been hoping that Mrs. Briggs would stay to help with the washing up, but in view of her shocked state Father offered to drive her home instead, and it wasn't long before she'd wrapped herself up again in her damp rain-cape and departed. While they were away Mother spoke to me again about the incident. "Becky, that was a shocking outburst of Mrs. Briggs's and I know it absolutely ruined the end of your party, but I'm sure the girls will remember the nice bits too when they get home."

"I expect so," I said meekly. I knew that Mother herself must be disappointed that none of the parents had stayed at the end for a chat.

"Now, the thing is," Mother said, "that Cora really is a

bit of a problem child—there've been all sorts of ongoings we knew nothing about. And Mrs. Briggs has been very closely involved. We mustn't hold this incident against her . . . And—well—I really think it'd be better if you didn't see Cora any more." She broke off abruptly and looked at me. I said nothing. "Do you think that's terribly unfair?" she asked.

"Of course I do," I said.

"Becky, look, we're new here. Don't let's be awkward customers straight away. See how the Spensers and the Phillipses and the Fosters couldn't wait to get out of the house when they saw Cora was here. How are we ever going to fit in if we keep having her round? We'll just be stuck with Cora and her father for company. How're you going to like that? I thought you liked the other girls. There'll be no more going round to Hermione's, you know, if you have Cora tagging on like a little shadow all the time."

I knew she was right and I knew that I didn't want to lose Hermione and the others. Furthermore, I had promised them faithfully that I'd cut Cora off at once. But that was when I thought she'd really done something wicked to Dory. It was all Mrs. Briggs's fault; if she hadn't leapt to hysterical conclusions and lost her head none of this would have happened. "All right, Mummy," I said. "I'll give Cora up. I'm not that keen on her anyway. But I do think it's unfair to her." It was true that in a way I found it difficult to be fond of Cora; her lapdog attitude to me was too irritating. There had been moments when she'd seemed less dependent on my approval and goodwill but so far these hadn't lasted. All the same, I was bothered by the total injustice of what everyone was demanding—that I should cut her off completely.

"It is a bit unfair," said Mother. "I'm not that happy about it myself, but I can't see any alternative. Not at the moment, anyway. Maybe later . . . if it all dies down . . . But at the moment you've got a new school to settle into and we've all got new friends to make. We must make an effort to fit in—there are the boys to consider as well."

On my way up to bed I saw Cora's little present lying unopened on the hall window-ledge. I must have shoved it there absent-mindedly when she arrived. I unwrapped it as I went upstairs. It contained two postcard-sized pieces of cardboard, and carefully sandwiched between them was a piece of paper which had obviously been carefully cut from a notebook. I turned it over and there was the most delicately painted forget-me-not that I had ever seen. The colours and details of petal and leaf were just right; it was exquisite. In the bottom corner was a clear signature— "Myra Ravenwing". Cora had included a little note: "Dear Becky, I wanted to give you some of Mum's roses on your birthday but you weren't happy about that so I hope you'll be happy with this instead. With love from your friend Cora." I stared at the little painting and felt strangely excited. Cora had actually taken scissors to one of her mother's diaries so that I could have it. What would her father say if he found out? What had she risked for my sake?

I lay for a long time after I'd got into bed just gazing at the flower propped up on my bedside table. When I heard Mother coming up to kiss me goodnight I instinctively seized it and hid it between the pages of the poetry book that Hermione had given me. Afterwards that seemed symbolic; that was what I'd have to do with Cora. *She'd* have to be secret. I would be openly friendly with Hermione and Susan and Barbara but secretly there would always be Cora.

When I lay down something dug into my wrist and I sat up again sharply and turned my bedside light on. Mrs. Briggs's hobgoblin glinted up from my arm in triumph—he'd done for my party all right! In rage I tore the bracelet off, opened my window and flung it out into the dark night. It wasn't found for weeks and by then it was so tarnished and rusty that I never had to wear it again, though Mother made me keep it to save Mrs. Briggs's feelings.

Chapter 7 ❀ The Hideout

THE NEXT DAY WAS SUNDAY AND THE NEW SCHOOL TERM was due to start on Tuesday, so there wasn't a lot of time to do what I finally decided would have to be done.

In the morning Mother was gratified to receive phone calls from the Phillipses, Fosters and Spensers saying how much the girls had enjoyed the party and how rude it must have seemed that none of them had stayed long enough to introduce themselves properly. Mrs. Phillips phoned first and Mother and Father agreed over lunch that it looked as if the others must have selected her as spokeswoman, for she was on the phone for a considerable length of time and took it upon herself to apprise Mother of some of the aspects of Cora's life which had led to her being, by now, totally ostracized by the community. Whatever Mother really thought she reacted to the news in the way she knew Mrs. Phillips would want her to. I sat out of sight at the top of the stairs and listened to her end of the conversation. ". . . Yes, quite, Sylvia . . . If I'd known . . . Mrs. Briggs

did tell us afterwards . . . No, Becky doesn't know . . .
we've decided it's best . . . yes . . . The others don't discuss
it? . . . Quite . . . No . . . I thought not . . . No, she's no
idea . . . No, she's not going to see her again. She can see
the others are upset by her—and she's very fond of Hermione, of course . . . Oh, she does? That's nice. Yes, they
enjoy it, don't they?''

So Hermione hadn't told her mother she'd told me all
about Cora! She must have decided to forgive me after all.
I'd been worrying about her continuing silence after the
other two had expressed their willingness to overlook the
blunder of inviting Cora to the party. Only Hermione had
sat remote, white and silent, undecided as to whether such
crassness on my part must rule me out as a suitable friend.
Now it seemed all was well. She'd concealed the full extent
of my knowledge from her parents and might even, from the
sound of it, have said she liked me, enjoyed our poetry
discussions . . . In the midst of my pleasure at seeing the
way clear again to being one of a foursome with the others
I did not overlook the fact that in order to tell her parents
the truth she'd have had to confess to gossiping to me about
Cora, a thing they'd expressly forbidden. But her motives
didn't bother me greatly. What I was overjoyed by was
the prospect of the new school term with her as my best
friend. It was more than I deserved after the tactlessness
of subjecting all three of them to an afternoon of Cora.

In the back of my mind, of course, nagging away so
persistently that it eventually worked its way to the fore,
was my feeling of guilt for what I had subjected Cora to.
And it was after I'd accepted this and recognized her complete blamelessness from the start of the party to its
catastrophic conclusion that I decided to do my best to
make things up to her. On Sunday afternoon, while Mother

and Father were gardening and thinking I was indoors listening to the wireless, I sneaked out of the house and went looking for her.

I was pretty sure that I knew where to find her and I was right. As I picked my way nervously round the side of the church, there she was, spreadeagled in the sunshine beside her mother's grave. She was staring up at the sky and didn't see me at first but continued singing some folk-song I didn't know in lark-like tones :

> "So bury me where the boughs hang low,
> And the sun-cast shadows come and go,
> And, 'neath the grass, while the seasons pass,
> I'll join the love that I long for so."

She sensed my presence, stopped abruptly, and sat up, rubbing her eyes and focusing on me. "Becky !"

"Hello, Cora ! I thought you'd be here."

"Mmmm."

"Cora, I'm sorry about that mess-up at the end of the party. And thank you so much for the painting."

"What d'you think of it ?"

"Beautiful."

"I chose her forget-me-not on purpose, you know."

"I guessed you might have."

"Yes. I don't want you to forget we're friends, whatever happens when school starts again."

"It's going to be hard, Cora. I promised the others I wouldn't speak to you again."

"Why did you do that ?"

"Well, I thought you'd done something bad to Dory. For a moment I believed all the stories about you. The others were so upset and hated me for asking you to the party at all."

"Oh, I thought they were almost putting up with me."

"I think they were at one stage, but then when Mrs. Briggs kicked up that hullaballoo . . ."

"Your Dad was very nice to me, you know."

"Yes, I'm not surprised. He stuck up for you after too. But it's no good. Mummy says I've got to get rid of you. She says she doesn't want us losing everybody's friendship on your account."

Cora shrugged. I thought this was a good place to be breaking all this bad news to her; she always had a special strength here. "Is that it, then?"

"Well, no. Perhaps it needn't be. But we can't be normal friends. I thought perhaps we could still be secret friends."

The idea seemed to appeal to her. She smiled mischievously. "You'll get yourself tied in awful knots, Becky," she said, "and if the others find out they'll hate you like anything!"

"Oh, I know," I said anxiously. "Are you trying to put me off? Do you think it's a bad idea?"

"Well, I don't think it's all that marvellous," she said bluntly. "Who'd want to be tucked in on the sly? I'd much rather you chose me rather than them. That would really be one in the eye . . ."

"I can't do that, Cora," I said. "Firstly I like them and secondly I've promised Mummy not to make things awkward . . ."

"O.K.," she said. "I'll take whatever's offered. I might as well. It's better than nothing. Now, tell me what Mrs. Briggs said after I'd gone."

"I don't know," I said. "Mummy and Daddy didn't want me to hear. They're quite fair really, you know. Mummy's only wanting to fit in here; it isn't that she believes you're bad."

"Mmmm."

"I think Mrs. Briggs got quite hysterical and told them you were . . . pretty bad . . ."

"A Devil Child. I bet that's what she said."

"Well—yes—something like that. I think it's dreadful, Cora. And I think you're very brave not to be terribly upset by her."

"I am," said Cora. "Upset, I mean."

"Oh, Cora. I am sorry. You've had such a rotten time," I said. "What does your father say?"

"Not much. He ignores people. Says he doesn't need them any more than they need him."

"Oh dear . . . By the way, why *did* you take Dory in the airing-cupboard?"

"We were hiding. He saw me go in and kept pulling at the door. I thought he'd give me away, so I just took him in beside me. He's so sweet—I love babies. We'd never have dozed off if you'd found us quicker."

"Mrs. Briggs thought you were trying to suffocate him."

"I know. Your father told me. He said it was a silly place to hide but not really dangerous. I knew that—there are ventilation holes in the door. I know all about oxygen and that—Actually he said I shouldn't be too upset because it was really all *your* fault."

"*My* fault!"

"Yes. He said he hadn't given you permission to start a game of hide-and-seek over the whole house and he never would have done. He just pretended to smack me on the bottom and sent me down to play with you lot."

"Well, he wouldn't realize the state the others were in. Susan was crying and Hermione went all white and trembly."

"She would! Oh, I knew that that would be the end of it.

Blast Mrs. Briggs! She's always going to wreck things for me, isn't she? She's a right witch herself—don't you think so?"

"I know what you mean. I hate her. But half the village seems to think she's someone special. Mummy quite likes her . . ."

"She's just a gossipy, malicious, old bag."

"Cora!"

"—And she's got it in for me. She hates me. She thinks I make people die. Everything I do, she twists it round to look as if I've meant harm. And people always believe her."

"I don't think they do really. Not deep down. But you can see how everything fits in . . . and she's terribly convincing."

I couldn't stay long. I didn't want Mother and Father to know I'd slipped away at all. We agreed not to acknowledge one another publicly, not to be friendly at school. Cora said it wouldn't be any different from usual for her, nobody at school ever was friendly except for one or two of the teachers. I said I'd talk to her whenever it was possible, whenever nobody was watching. That sounded so grudging and mean that I promised to try and come to some sort of arrangement whereby we might meet privately in the evenings or something. I left her humming to herself and stroking the grass idly with the back of her hand. I stopped to wave as I went round the side of the church and she waved back as if nothing were amiss. I felt unkind and unfair—I had offered her a crumb of friendship and she'd accepted it as better than nothing. But she deserved far more than that.

On Tuesday school started. I dressed up in my brand-new uniform—Mother had even bought me new underwear— and was so excited that I couldn't manage much breakfast. The uniform was beige and blue; beige blouse, blue gym-slip, beige and blue striped tie, and a blue cardigan with beige stripes round the cuffs. There was a blue tweed coat and a blue velours hat for wearing outside. The whole lot had been rather expensive and Mother had bought everything on the big side to allow for growth, but I still felt very smart. Mother said she'd take me, as it was the first day, but we met Hermione as we passed the bottom of her drive and I sent Mother home as I felt I didn't need her. She looked a bit abashed and I realized then that she'd really wanted to take me. Anyway, she said goodbye, and Hermione and I went on to school together, talking and smiling and becoming best friends. There was a moment of awkwardness as we passed the end of the road that led up to St. Matthew's Church and the common. Cora was running down the hill, coat flapping. She could easily have joined us, but we both deliberately ignored her and carried on talking to each other. Hermione was undoubtedly relieved at my reaction, but neither of us said anything. Cora eventually overtook us and ran on ahead to school. She didn't turn to look at me once.

Hermione showed me where to hang my coat and then we went to our form-room. There were seventeen in the class and most of them seemed to have arrived already. There was much banging of desks and noisy argument between any who wanted the same one. Barbara had arrived early and claimed a block of four beside one of the windows towards the front of the class. She and Susan were to have the front two and the two behind were reserved for Hermione and me. The desks were of dark brown wood and had inkwells and heavy lids with initials scratched and carved into them. Miss Dingwall called me to the front after a while and welcomed me. Then to my embarrassment she hushed the class to introduce me officially.

"This is Rebecca Stokes," she said. "She's joining us this

term and I hope we're all going to help her settle in very quickly."

I blushed and looked round the roomful of blank faces. Only Barbara and Hermione were smiling helpfully. Susan was giggling at my discomfort and Cora, in the least popular desk right under the teacher's nose, was staring at me unblinking with her sharp, black eyes. It was the first time she had looked at me; I suppose she thought it would be safe to as everyone else would be.

"You can sit down now, Rebecca," said Miss Dingwall. "I imagine they've all taken you in."

The rest of the morning was occupied with assignment of cloakroom peg numbers, pens, nibs, pencils, checks on name-tapes and dictation of the time-table. There were breaks for milk at eleven and lunch at a quarter to one. We started lessons in the afternoon with English, taught by Miss Dingwall, and Scripture, taught by Miss Todd, the headmistress. At the end of the lesson she called me to the front as the others packed up for the day and started to leave. She said a lot of polite things about being pleased to have me at the school and hoping I'd soon feel at home, and I smiled politely too, and said: "Thank you."

That was it! The first day over. Hermione and the others had lingered behind for me and we went along and put on our coats together. I was looking forward to the walk home. I wondered if Barbara or Susan would ask me in for a bit before tea as I hadn't been to their houses yet and I knew they both lived in the village. But Mother was waiting at the school gate. I felt terribly angry with her. I didn't want to see her at all. Of course the others all smiled and said, "Hello, Mrs. Stokes. Goodbye, Becky, see you to-morrow," and hurried off together. I was left with Mother.

"You didn't need to meet me."

"I thought on the first day . . ."

"Look, they've all gone off now. I wanted to be with them."

"I'm sorry, dear. You'll see them tomorrow. How did it go?"

I couldn't be bothered telling her a thing. Trust her to come fussing round!

There was the sound of pattering feet overtaking from behind. "Hello, Mrs. Stokes." It was Cora, not stopping or hanging on, just passing the time of day in a friendly fashion.

Mother jumped. "Oh, hello, Cora, dear. Did you enjoy your first day back?" she said, trying to be friendly but not actually stopping.

"Yes, thank you," said Cora. She trotted on past us.

"I hope she hasn't been hanging round you all day," whispered Mother.

"No, she hasn't. I haven't spoken to her at all if you want to know."

Suddenly Mother lost her temper. "You can really be a selfish little brat, Becky. You nasty, mean girl to treat me to this temper when I've been thinking about you all day and hoping things were going well."

"I didn't need to be met. You've just got in the way."

"Well, I certainly shan't again! It's a lot of bother parking the boys somewhere for half an hour—and I'd much rather have their company than yours when you're like this!" I think she'd have stormed off and left me, but she looked round first, not wanting our row to be observed, and Miss Todd was approaching with the deputy head. They stopped to exchange greetings and welcomes and Mother and I had to stop glaring at each other and simper. After they had gone, I apologized for being mean and gave Mother a detailed account of the day, including the lunch menu. She was particularly interested in that.

The term seemed to get quickly under way after that first fragmented sort of a day, and I soon found that I was well up to standard academically. My favourite lessons were English and gym. I was always keen and attentive in those, but my concentration wavered a fair amount in the other lessons and I doodled with bits of poetry and wrote notes to Susan, trying to make her laugh. Hermione and Barbara were fairly strait-laced and good during class but Susan and I notched up one or two order marks and detentions as the term went on, nothing too disgraceful though.

There was one very naughty girl in the class. Her name was Georgia Jamieson. I didn't like her very much as she seemed such a show-off, but she could be very funny and cheeky, and I often found myself hoping she'd start up some sort of diversion to get us all through a particularly tedious lesson. Once I found her all swollen and blotched in the cloakroom. She'd been sent to the headmistress by Miss Bayliss, the art teacher, who'd finally had enough of her insolence and tomfoolery. Some time later I had asked permission to fetch a hanky from my coat pocket in the cloakroom, and there was Georgia, sobbing away, her face buried in her coat. I was absolutely amazed. I couldn't understand how she could carry on being naughty if she was so upset by the resulting rows and trouble.

"What's wrong, Georgia?"

"Nothing. Miss Todd said awful things, that's all." She brought her wet face out from her coat. Her eyes were very red and her breath came in gasps.

"What things?"

"Oh, that they were all sick of me, she wished she'd

never taken me into the school, I was a menace, other parents had complained . . ."

"Oh, Georgia! That's awful!"

"I'm not so bad, am I?"

"Well, I don't think so. But the teachers do seem to get irritated. Perhaps you should make a real effort to be good."

"I do try—but I never seem to manage it. They pick on me a bit."

"I suppose they're expecting you to do something bad all the time—I'll have to go, Miss Bayliss'll be wondering where I am. Are you coming back to art?"

"No, I don't want to see anyone like this. I'll go and wash my face." By the time she rejoined the class for the next lesson she looked just the same as usual. I had the utmost difficulty convincing Hermione and Barbara and Susan of the state that the irrepressible Georgia had been in in the cloakroom.

"She gets my goat a bit," said Hermione. "She overdoes it all the time. It's not really all that funny."

"Mummy says she'll get herself expelled if she doesn't look out," said Barbara. "Mummy and Daddy met her parents one parents' night. They're very nice and it's a great mystery to them why Georgia's always in trouble. Mrs. Jamieson told Mummy she dreads the parents' nights because she never knows what she's going to hear next."

Cora, to my surprise, was very quiet and industrious at school. She seemed to be quite a favourite with the teachers. They didn't appear to share the local hostility to her at all. I wondered if they knew what a sad and difficult life she'd had and if they were trying to compensate her in some way. At any rate, she didn't cause any difficulties in class and at breaks just kept herself to herself. If I hadn't seen and heard all I had during the holidays it would have taken

me weeks to notice her at all. As it was, I was fairly well
aware of her most of the time and it wasn't very long
before we began to exchange a few covert glances. After
about ten days I found a note from her in my desk.

"Shall we meet?" it said. "Say when and where."

The obvious time to suggest was Thursday, after my
piano lesson. I stayed late at school for that; all the other
days I had taken to walking home with my three special
friends. I suggested one of the old air-raid shelters in a field
near the school for our secret meeting place. There were
about a dozen shelters in the field. They were half sunk
into the ground and entered by steps at one end or an iron
ladder through a hole in the roof at the other. I don't know
why they had been left standing. The field couldn't be
ploughed because of the huge hummocks they made on the
surface of the ground; cows were grazed there sometimes.

I felt strangely nervous and excited as I darted out of
school after my piano lesson and ran down the hill towards the field. It was a sunny day, birds were singing
loudly and the hedgerows were still thick and green and
flowery. There was nobody about. I threw my music-case
and satchel over the five-bar gate and began to climb over
myself, pausing at the top to scan the field for Cora. She
wasn't in sight. She must be in one of the shelters but I
didn't know which; I foolishly hadn't specified any particular one. I didn't like the field; the grass was long and full of
nettles and thistles, and the bumps made by the shelters
looked like giant graves. I'd only been in once before, with
Hermione and the others. The shelters were dark inside and
it took moments to adjust to the gloom; drops of moisture
constantly seeped through the arched roofs and splattered
on the floor. Hermione said her mother said they weren't
safe, as odd bricks had started to fall out of the ceilings. I

always wondered if madmen or murderers might lurk there
and usually scurried past at top speed on Thursdays when
I was on my own. I imagined the war, and the terror of
bombers going over—screaming women and children, ex-
plosions, blood everywhere! In fact, I believe the shelters
were scarcely used at all and only one stray bomb landed
on Okefield during the course of the entire war.

I wished desperately that I had had the sense to tell Cora
exactly where to wait for me and almost thought of
abandoning the meeting and going on home. But it didn't
seem fair to leave her sitting alone in one of these dark,
derelict tunnels, so I gingerly retrieved my music-case and
satchel and picked my way through the tough, weedy grass
to the entrance of the nearest shelter. I hurried down the
steep brick steps and peered in. I couldn't see a thing.
"Cora," I whispered into the pitch blackness. No answer.
Just the noise of my own breathing and the nervous pump-
ing of my heart as I paused for a few seconds. Then up the
steps I dashed and on to the next shelter. I was becoming
terrified by my own imaginings. The grass was so tall I
could hardly struggle through it. What if someone jumped
up suddenly and grabbed me? I was getting further and
further away from the lane; nobody would hear my
screams. Cora wasn't in the second shelter or the third. I
was almost sobbing with fear as I emerged the third time
and looked around.

"Coo-eee! . . . Becky!" Across the field came her bright,
clear voice. There she was! I caught sight of her dark little
head sticking up out of one of the shelters like a sweep's
brush. In a flash I felt completely recovered. No maniacs
sneaking through the long grass to club me down, just
Cora waiting patiently and, no doubt, very pleased that I'd
come. I made my way over to her and clambered up the

slope to where she was standing at the top of the ladder leading down the "chimney" of the shelter.

"I like these ladders, don't you? Much more fun than the steps."

"I've never tried one of the ladders, actually."

"Oh. Well, come on in." Cora disappeared down inside the chimney and I climbed inside after her and started to feel my way down. There were only fifteen rungs down to the floor of the shelter. To my surprise, Cora had lit the place with candles and I had no difficulty seeing when I got down.

"Golly! You've made this super, Cora." She'd brought some bright old rugs and cushions and pictures and made a little secret hideout for us at one end of the shelter.

"Do you like it? I thought if we were going to meet here regularly it ought to be nice. We couldn't just sit shivering in the dark."

"No. It's smashing. Actually I was a bit frightened out there just now when I was looking for you. I was wishing like mad that I hadn't suggested this field. But now I think it was a good idea. Did you bring all these things today?"

It turned out that Cora had actually put a lot of thought and work into planning our secret den. The day I'd planted my reply to her note in her desk she'd come to the field by herself and inspected all the shelters. This one was in the best state of repair, the least damp and musty. She thought we migh be able to leave the rugs and cushions here without them getting covered in mildew. She hoped I'd agree to this being our permanent *rendez-vous*. Perhaps we could meet every Thursday. I was taken by surprise by Cora taking command like this and excited by the aspects of secrecy surrounding the arrangement—my secret friend, our secret den, our secret meetings. My earlier fear heightened the thrill of it all. "Oh Cora," I whispered as the candles flickered, throwing strange shadows on the damp, brick walls around us, "you're very clever! It's a terrific little hideout. Nobody'll ever find us. Yes, let's meet every Thursday."

Then Cora triumphantly pulled a bag of crisps and a bottle of lemonade out of her satchel. "Let's celebrate," she said, and we lingered there for about half an hour, eating, talking about school, and planning further improvements for the shelter. I felt as if I was in the middle of an adventure story and later, as we picked our way back across the field, I rather enjoyed frightening myself with fearful imaginings and striding on regardless with Cora by my side. At the gate we parted. Cora decided to let me go on ahead in case we should meet someone accidentally. I raced home in time for tea and told Mother that the piano lesson had lasted longer than usual and then I'd been delayed by school friends I'd met in the lane. She didn't mind in the least.

"It's a friendly little place, isn't it, Becky? Just as long as you're always back in time for tea . . ."

Chapter 8 ❧ The Concert

I FOUND LIFE TOTALLY PLEASING FOR JUST ABOUT THE WHOLE
of that first term at Okington School. Hermione and I enjoyed each other's company every day at school and most
weekends we met at each other's houses and read our poetry,
went walks and had tea together. Several times she took me
back to Paradise and, while the summer lasted, we picnicked
there and enjoyed the secrecy and solitude. I never felt
smug or deceitful about the fact that I had another secret
place that she wasn't privy to. Looking back, it seems surprising that I didn't feel guilty or dishonest in my dealings
with her, but I didn't. I just kept the two friendships totally
separate in my mind and valued both of them. In fact, I
was much more honest with Cora, although I saw consider-
ably less of her. There was nothing I couldn't say to her.
She knew all about my activities with Hermione—posh teas
at Stansfield House, poetry readings, Paradise. I think she
thought it all rather affected and silly, but she didn't scoff;
she accepted the fact that I was impressed by the Phillips

set-up and wanted to be a part of it. I don't think I was a snob or a social climber and I don't really think my mother was either (although she did seem to relish my friendship with Hermione). I would have envied Hermione's frail beauty and heightened sensitivity even if she'd been as poor as a church mouse. And I wouldn't have treated Cora any differently if she'd been rich; given otherwise identical circumstances we'd still have ended up in our secret alliance.

After half-term, activities at school began to centre on the Christmas concert. Apparently Okington School put one on every year and the parents always enjoyed it very much and were very impressed. There were various instrumental solos, and the junior and senior choirs sang selections of songs, and there were recorder groups, a percussion band, various bits of elocution and choral speaking. I was in the junior choir and a recorder group, and Barbara and I were selected to play a piano duet together, so I felt very much a part of the whole programme and threw myself into extra rehearsals with gusto. Mother and Father seemed very pleased that I was so involved and were looking forward to furthering the acquaintance of other parents at the interval and afterwards.

One or two of the girls in our class weren't included in a single item on the programme, and I thought they must feel very depressed about that. Georgia Jamieson, who could actually sing very nicely, had been thrown out of the choir for giggling and talking and was in nothing else, and Anne Price, a weakly, chesty girl, who was always off school, wasn't in anything either. I must say I thought it very game when I heard they were intending to come on the night just to listen to the rest of us. Hermione said Mr. and Mrs. Jamieson would be dragging Georgia there by the hair of her head, and we'd probably all be better off if she didn't come as she'd be bound to be disruptive in some way. I think Hermione was particularly anxious as she'd been chosen to recite some of her own poetry and she wanted everyone to pay attention. It would be just like Georgia to create a disturbance; the sight or sound of anything pretentious did tend to bring out the worst in her. All the same, with a Jamieson parent on either side of her, I didn't really think there'd be a squeak out of Georgia and I just felt sorry for her. At least Anne Price had been considered responsible enough to help with selling programmes and serving coffee at the interval, but nobody was going to risk giving Georgia a chance to be included in any way at all.

I was secretly very envious of Hermione for getting a chance to perform as a poetess. I wished it was going to be me and yet I could see that she certainly looked more the part. When she was reciting she would cast her blue eyes around so wistfully and sometimes pull thoughtfully at one of her curls. Then she would reel off a perfect description of a bluebell wood or snow-clad mountains or a stormy night sky or something, all composed by herself. I was certain she would be the star of the evening. I consoled myself with the thought that I really looked far too pink and rosy to be a poetess and people might find it rather hilarious if I publicly set myself up as one.

Cora, who'd seen some of my poems by now and thought them quite nice, did break her silence about Hermione's poetry during one of our Thursday meetings. The days had become cold by this time and the air-raid shelter was pretty uncomfortable, but we liked to be certain of our half-hour together on Thursdays, so we still met there every week and huddled, side by side, in the candle-light, wrapped in our damp rugs.

"I think your poetry's better than Hermione's."

"Oh rubbish! You're just saying that to please me. Hers is frightfully atmospheric."

"Just frightful if you ask me! It's so artificial. And the way she recites it . . . I think she's a scream."

"Well, you must be odd, then. Nobody else finds her amusing."

"Don't they just! You should see Georgia Jamieson taking her off!"

"Oh, well—*Georgia*! I'd expect her to make fun of any-body who was trying to be serious."

"Georgia's not as bad as all that."

"What d'you mean?"

"She's like me in a way. People have made their minds up against her. She's an outcast . . ."

"Oh, look, you can't deny she's awfully naughty. She asks for it."

"She doesn't mean to, though. She says she can't stop."

"Are you friends with her, Cora?"

"No, not really. We've had one or two talks, but she's not really allowed to talk to me."

"Who says?"

"Her parents. She'll get a beating if she does."

"A beating!"

"Her dad beats her up."

"Don't be ridiculous! You're exaggerating!"

"I'm not, you know."

"That mild little man! He couldn't swat a fly."

"He more than swats Georgia. He leathers her."

"But everyone says he's so nice . . ."

"Well, everyone says Mrs. Briggs is nice, but see what she's done to me."

I was absolutely thunderstruck and could hardly think of anything else for several days. Poor Georgia! What horrible lives she and Cora led. It seemed grossly unfair that my life should be so unproblematical and pleasant in comparison. It was frustrating not being able to discuss what I'd heard with anyone at all. It was obvious that Georgia had confided in Cora because of a sense of their mutual experience of misery and loneliness. Although Georgia was constantly surrounded by a group of girls laughing at her antics and enjoying her displays, when the show was over they vanished. Nobody wanted to be too closely associated with her "performances" for fear of incurring a share of the wrath which usually followed. In any case, it was actually very difficult to know what Georgia was really like behind the clownish exterior.

I did attempt to hint to Hermione that the Jamieson parents might not be all they seemed, but she was puzzled and sceptical of the idea.

"What on earth are you on about? They're *terribly* nice. Mummy and Daddy have had them to cocktails and all sorts."

I wished I could tell her what Cora had said, but everyone assumed I'd severed relations with her completely. "She's got odd bruises sometimes. I've seen them when we've been changing for gym."

"Becky! You can't go around suggesting that sort of thing. You'll get into awful trouble. Why don't you ask Georgia, anyway?"

"You can't go up to someone and say 'Did your father beat you last night?' "

"I don't see why not. If he had she'd probably be quite pleased to go on about it."

"I don't think it works like that. If Daddy hit me, really hard I mean, I wouldn't be in a rush to tell you about it."

"Why not?"

"I'd rather pretend I had as nice a father as you. Even if he was horrible I'd still rather you thought he was nice."

"How odd." Hermione paused and thought about it. "Mmm. All the same, I wouldn't let Barbara hear you saying all this. Her parents are very pally with the Jamiesons and if Barbara told them what you'd said they'd be furious with you."

So the whole thing got hushed up and Georgia carried on being naughty and getting into bad trouble all the time. Once I tried to be friendly but she was rather abrupt with me. I think she was ashamed of the fact that I'd seen her in the cloakroom that day, all the defences down, tears streaming down her wretched face.

During the last month before the concert, Barbara and I were frequent visitors to each other's houses. We were determined that our little piano duet, which came quite early in the programme, should be absolutely flawless. I was playing the top part, which was very fast in places, and Barbara was playing the bottom part, with a lot of heavy chords, although sometimes she took over the tune while I just played frilly bits way up high.

I enjoyed going to the Fosters'. They lived in a neat little modern house on the outskirts of the village and Mrs. Foster, who sometimes worked nights as a nurse at the local hospital, kept the place spotless. It was always clean and fresh-smelling and bright, unlike my own home which was basically clean enough but rarely immaculate. As Mother was always saying in self-defence, it was a hopeless task trying to clean up after Jo and Dory, and she would drive herself insane if she didn't relax standards while they were little. I don't remember standards tightening all that much as we grew up, and none of us minded or I suppose we'd have done something about it ourselves, but the light airiness of the Fosters' house made a nice change. I was too young then to care much about the architectural superiorities of our older house. I would have been equally happy in a contemporary semi-detached house on an estate.

Barbara had a twin brother, Derek, who was great fun. There were no other children in the family and the two were a very devoted pair. I could see why Barbara remained unflustered by most events at school, the ups and down of Hermione's moods, Susan's scattiness, my arrival in the gang. She was very fond of us all and a loyal, stalwart friend, but her home life was what mattered most to her, and Derek in particular. He had a freckly face like hers and the same sandy, wavy hair. He used to go off and kick a ball around their small garden while Barbara and I practised our duet and then, when he thought we'd been at it long enough, he'd come in in his stockinged feet, fling himself full-length on the sofa and try to make us laugh.

Once, when I was at the Fosters', and Barbara and I had practised enough and stopped for tea, Mrs. Foster sat down beside us with her cup of tea and started to chat. We talked about the duet and the concert for quite a while. Then Mrs. Foster said: "Well, then, Becky—it's nearly the end of your first term. What do you think of Okington?"

"I love it."

"Do you still miss your old school?"

"Not really—some of my friends I do a bit. But . . ."

"Mmm. Okington does seem nice. Barbara has always enjoyed it, haven't you, love? Nearly everyone seems happy with the place. No misfits really—just Cora Ravenwing and little Georgia, I suppose." I started guiltily at Cora's name and went pink. Mrs. Foster was watching me closely. "Don't worry, dear, about your little mistake with Cora. Everyone has forgotten all about it now. And you couldn't possibly

have been expected to know what she was like. Oh, dear—
it's a pity, really, that there have to be children like that—
just bad all through." I felt enraged on Cora's behalf and
wanted to protest but I didn't dare and Mrs. Foster moved
on before I had time to pluck up courage. "And little
Georgia. Well, she's a real puzzle. What the Jamiesons have
done to deserve her I don't know. But the breeding is there
—so we must assume she'll turn out all right in the end."

I saw my chance. "Perhaps Cora will be all right in the
end too."

She turned sharply. "No chance of that, dear. The difference between her and Georgia is quite clear. Cora's a completely rotten apple but Georgia has just lost her way a bit,
that's all."

I didn't like Mrs. Foster so much after that. She seemed
hard and cold. I hoped I wouldn't ever end up in hospital
being nursed by her. And her super-efficient house-cleaning
began to seem less attractive too. She'd scour and scrub and
polish and hoover all the time I was there. But there was no
doubt of her pride in Barbara and Derek. They were the
ones she laboured for. She was going to give them the
chances she and Mr. Foster had never had. He was there
only once when I went to practise. He was a representative
for some carpet-manufacturing firm and he came plodding
in at seven o'clock just as I was leaving. He looked very
weary, but took a friendly interest in me and persuaded
me to take my coat off again and play through the duet
with Barbara, just for him. He was terribly impressed when
we'd finished and said it was marvellous . . .

The concert was to be held in a hall in Heatherton, a
market town near Okefield. This was the procedure every
year. It was thought that the audience would be too big to
fit in the school hall, so we were decamping to a real hall

with dimming lights in the auditorium, spotlights on stage, and a curtain. I'd never known anything like it and felt very excited, though the others enjoyed pretending to be unaffected by the scurry of arrangements as we were ferried to and fro for rehearsals in the hall. Lessons were well and truly disrupted for the best part of a week as individuals were required to leave classrooms and gather at the school gate to get into the green coach that seemed to be at our disposal. "Oh, you get used to it, you know," said Hermione loftily as I sat, during a wet dinner-hour, nose pressed to the window, watching the senior choir filing across the asphalt to board the bus. "Once you've been through it all one year it doesn't seem so special the next time. Isn't that right, Barb?"

Barbara agreed that it was nothing to get too worked up about. "All the same, I could feel a bit wobbly about our duet—just Becky and me on stage under the spotlight . . ."

"Oh, Barb! Honestly! Well it's not going to throw me," said Hermione.

I nudged Susan and said: "She's in a frightful state really; look at her thumb nails." Susan laughed and Hermione, who'd been tidying her desk, slammed the lid down, glared at me and stalked out.

Susan stopped laughing. "That was a bit mean, Becky. I think you've really upset her."

"Well, she's so sneery sometimes. It gets me down."

Barbara said: "I expect she was only trying to convince herself about not getting over-excited. She's pretty jumpy."

"Oh blast!" I said. "I can see you think I ought to go and apologize."

"I'll come too," said Susan. "I was as bad laughing."

"Oh, no, you stay here," I said crossly. "It was my fault. I'll do the crawling."

I found Hermione on a bench in the cloakroom, weeping. "Oh, I'm sorry, Hermione," I said. "I didn't mean to be rotten. I shouldn't have said about your nails. Nobody notices anyway and certainly the audience isn't going to."

Hermione dabbed at her eyes and looked at me coldly. "I'm not that vain," she said. "I'm more grieved at your betrayal. How could you be so unfeeling?—I wouldn't have thought you had it in you."

"Oh, I'm not all that sensitive, really," I retorted, still cross. "You're the poetess, not me."

"Are you jealous, Becky? Is that why you went for me?"

"Oh, a bit, I expect," I said sheepishly. "And you were being a bit superior, you know, with all that stuff about how it wasn't particularly special to be performing on a real stage."

"Well, if you really want to know, I'm terrified!" she admitted suddenly.

"Oh, me too, Hermione!" I gasped, and in no time we were sitting there, side by side, holding our breath, hugging our knees, letting waves of delicious panic sweep us away together and squeaking that we'd just never manage. Then Hermione pulled herself together, straightened her gymslip and said sagely: "That'll have done us the world of good, you know, Becky, letting off steam like that."

"I suppose it will."

"Actually, it's better to be nervous. It makes for a more artistic performance. The most sensitive people are always nervous—it's only unfeeling clods who never feel a thing."

We were friends again. The excitement of the concert ran through me like shivers for days on end. I was totally happy. The day of the concert dawned at last. We were given the afternoon off school and instructed to be at the hall in Heatherton by quarter to seven. The programme started at seven and it was up to each individual to make her way back-stage at least two items before her own appearance. Mrs. Briggs was babysitting for Dory, and Jo was coming with Mother and Father and me. He was almost as excited about coming as I was about performing and Mother and Father got quite snappy with us on the way. I was worried that my fingers would never warm up in time for the duet, which was item number three. Mother sat in the back of the car beside me chafing them between hers all the way to Heatherton, while Jo bounced about in the front seat next to Father, knocking the gear lever and hand-brake with his knees. Father threatened to turn the car round and go home if he couldn't sit still, but we all knew those were empty words.

"Your hands feel warm as toast to me," said Mother. "You're making a fuss."

"It's just on the outside they're warm," I said. "They're chilled through . . . Oh! Where's my music?"

"Daddy's got it in front."

"Oh, thank Heavens!—Oh, I hope there'll be time to go to the lavatory."

"Of course there will be. Do you really need . . .? You've just been."

"Well, I need to go again."

"So do I," said Jo."

"Nobody's bothered about you," I snapped. "You're not performing."

I felt a lot better after we arrived, and Mother and Father found good seats and draped my coat over the one beside them so that I could sit with them when not required elsewhere. I scuttled back-stage and found Barbara already sitting there amongst the gathering hordes of the percussion band and a choral-speaking group. The youngest of the band would have been no more than seven and excitement was nearly getting the better of some of them despite the music mistress's soothing tones. She came and asked Barbara and me to help organize and equip the various sections with their instruments, and we forgot ourselves briefly in the business of sorting out triangles and cymbals and drum-sticks. Then it was time to begin, and they all trooped away, leaving us alone with the choral speakers, who were muttering to themselves, *sotto voce*, and striking their brows in agony as some line or other momentarily escaped them. Then they were gone and we were joined by people who would be going on stage after us.

And then it was our turn. Someone opened the door, beckoned us out, and we stole into the wings just as the choral speakers were finishing. We waited there with Miss Todd while they smiled and bowed to endless applause . . . And we waited while they left the stage the other side . . . And we waited while two fathers, who'd volunteered to assist, pushed forward the grand piano . . . And we waited while some silly parents thought it amusing to applaud *them*. My hands were clammy by now and my knees wobbling. Then, just as I'd decided to turn and run for it, Miss Todd, who'd had a comforting hand resting in the smalls of our backs, gave us a sudden push and said: "Off you go!" And we walked on. Clapping started at once, and we stood side by side and bowed, and then sat down and arranged our stools in the total silence that followed. And then we just started and after a few bars I knew it was sounding lovely. I began to enjoy myself as never before. My fingers danced in all the right places and Barbara's chords plodded beefily around at the bottom. I began to wish the piece was twice as long as it was. I wanted to be on stage for hours. Then and there I decided to scrap poetry and become a concert pianist. We reached the end, and, as our hands bounced up from the final chord, applause cracked out from all sides. We shook hands, bowed several times, and walked off. I could hardly bring myself to step out of the limelight.

In the wings, Barbara said: "Not bad!"

"Not bad! We were *tremendous*!" I seized her by both hands and spun her round.

"Rebecca Stokes, control yourself. You're not the only performer this evening," snapped the history teacher, pointing on stage to where a recorder group was already assembled, whistles to lips.

I wasn't very crushed, though, and Barbara and I bustled euphorically away and found a dim passage to rave in before we made our way to the auditorium to sit with our parents for a while. Mother and Father were both shiny-eyed and thrilled at how well I'd done but gave me only muted praise lest eavesdropping parents round about should think them over-indulgent. A lady behind leaned forward and whispered: "Beautiful, dear" in my ear. I sat in a haze of glory while other performers came and went and, to my shame, scarcely heard a word or note of what was going on . . . until the last item before the interval. This was Hermione's spot.

A senior girl, who'd been playing a terribly difficult piece by Beethoven, went off to a tremendous burst of applause; then one of the assisting fathers brought forward a small cane chair and placed it at the front of the apron-stage; then he disappeared and, after a few seconds, on came Hermione, just herself, in blouse and gymslip, no notes or exercise books or anything. Everyone craned forward to take in this delicate little slip of a thing. "Hermione Phillips recites her own work," the programme simply stated. She sat down, straight and composed, clasped her hands on her knees and crossed her feet at the ankles. The chair had been so positioned that she wasn't facing the audience straight on; we had a three-quarter view of her as she cleared her throat, lifted her head, gazed towards a far corner of the auditorium and began to speak. As she proceeded she became more animated, screwed her face up as if searching for words to describe her feelings, swept her pale brow with the back of a hand, tossed her curls. I thought it all most moving. She was brilliant. The compositions and the performance were flawless. Certainly, when she'd finished, there was a good deal of clapping. I just looked at Mother and sighed: "Isn't she marvellous!"

Mother said through her own loud clapping: "Very good indeed."

But, when we all rose and thought about shuffling into the foyer for coffee and biscuits, I heard the lady behind say to her friend: "What an affected little piece! Clever, though, I suppose."

"A right madam, I imagine!" said the friend and then they started chatting on some other topic.

I could hardly contain my indignation. Hadn't they listened to the poems at all? Hadn't Hermione's phrases and tones won through to them? I looked round, expecting other parents to be still breathless from the impact of the verses but, to all intents and purposes, not only her performance but the entire first half of the concert might never have occurred. The red velvet curtain now closed off the stage, and parents, almost in relief, were turning away from it and heading for the exits, hailing friends, waving, smiling, and searching pockets for coffee money and cigarettes. I felt very flattened for a second, but suddenly a little warm hand slid into mine and I looked down into Jo's round, pink, overawed face.

"It's terribly good, Becky," he said. "And you were wonderful!"

"Oh, Jo! You are nice. Did you really think so?"

"Oh, yes. People round about were clapping ever so hard and saying nice things. Mummy cried a bit, though."

"*Cried!*"

"She wiped her eyes."

"You ass, Jo! That's not proper crying. That means she thought I'd done well."

My spirits soared again. I tapped Father on the shoulder. "What did you really, truly, think of Barbara and me?" I whispered, so that nobody else in the mob squeezing its way down the centre gangway could possibly hear.

"Very, very good," he said firmly. "Mummy and I were terribly proud."

I glowed. "And what did you think of Hermione?" I whispered.

He paused. "I'm not terribly good on poetry," he said. "You should ask your mother. But it was a nice idea to have it on the programme. Made a nice little change."

"Mummy," I whispered, surprised at his response, "what did you think of Hermione?"

"Nice, love. But not a patch on you; the duet was really lovely."

In the foyer we met lots of other girls and parents. The Fosters pushed their way over, trying to shield joggling coffee cups. "Didn't the girls do well?" said Mrs. Foster, and Barbara and I shrugged and smiled. The Phillipses were there too, with two of the brothers and Horti. "Bright lass you've got there," said Father to Mr. Phillips. Mr. Phillips beamed broadly: "Runs in the family, sir," he said. And then he clapped Barbara and me on the shoulders. "Bravely played, girls! A masterly performance!"

Hermione was nowhere to be seen and eventually, despite my reluctance to forego further congratulations on my own performance from the thronging parents, I whispered to Barbara: "Let's go and find Hermione. I've a feeling her poetry didn't go down all that well. Perhaps she knows."

"It was O.K., wasn't it?" said Barbara.

"Well, I thought so, but other people don't seem to be as impressed as I thought they would be."

"Some people just don't go for poetry, of course . . ."

We took Jo back-stage with us. I thought he should have a bit of a treat, and it didn't seem fair to leave him stranded with a crowd of adults. He was glad to come, but clung tightly to my hand. We found Hermione sitting on the floor in the same passage where we'd skipped about in delight at our earlier success. She looked limp and downcast. I ran straight up and said buoyantly: "Well done, Hermione! It was terrific!"

She looked up hesitantly. "Was it really all right, Becky?"

"Course it was. You looked so poised and we could hear every word and you know I think your poetry's brilliant."

She stopped biting her nails and stood up slowly. "Hello, Jo," she said, seeing him. "It's late for you, isn't it?"

Jo nodded. "You were very good," he said shyly. "Mummy said so to Becky. I heard her."

That pleased her. "Really?" she said. "Oh, I'm so glad. I'd rather lost my nerve. I just felt too embarrassed to face anyone."

"You silly," I said. "It's lovely having all the parents praising you, isn't it, Barb?"

"Quite nice," admitted Barbara modestly.

Then Hermione remembered that we had also performed.

"Oh, you two were splendid," she said hastily. "No mistakes at all, were there?"

"I don't think there were," said Barbara, "though I thought we were going to lose the time at one stage."

"Oh, yes!" I agreed. "Just for a tiny minute when the slow bit ends and it gets fast again. What a panic! But we were O.K. I don't think anyone noticed."

"Oh, no. I don't think so."

Susan came dashing along the passage. "There you all are! I've been looking everywhere." I hadn't seen Susan earlier during the evening as we hadn't been on stage together. But the recorder group was first on after the interval. We were both in that.

"Hi, Sue! Is it time for us yet?"

"More or less." She panted up. "Well done, everyone! It's been super so far and you were all marvellous. Mummy and Daddy say they don't know how I come to have such talented friends!"

"Well, we can't begin to paint like you," said Barbara, to make up.

"Oh, don't worry, Barb. I'm not feeling small. I've enjoyed it all, honestly." She obviously had.

"You're a real good sport, Sue," I said.

"Well, it's my turn now, isn't it?" she said. "Come on, Becky—I think we should get ready now. I don't want to miss my go under the spotlight!"

Hermione and Barbara said they'd take Jo back to Mother and Father and offered him one hand each. He thought they were wonderful.

The second half went very smoothly and pleasantly and for most of it I sat with Mother and Father and told them little anecdotes about the performers. Towards the end I had to steal away back-stage because I was in the last item

—a stirring effort by the massed voices of both the senior and junior choirs. The whole lot of us crowded into the wings just before the penultimate item, which I'd been quite curious about, though not unduly as I wasn't involved. "Local Folk Music," the programme called it.

The silence which had always fallen between items after the applause had died down became absolutely total as, of all people, Cora Ravenwing stepped forward. But the quality of that silence had changed—it had been expectant, hopeful, encouraging, for all the other performers, but now it seemed hostile and negative. My heart began to pound quite painfully. How could Cora begin to do anything in this atmosphere? What was going to happen? Might someone shout abuse or even hurl something at her?

Cora walked quite briskly right to the front of the apron-stage and stood there, face on to the crowd. And then she started to sing. And her voice was beautiful. Every note was pure and true; her phrasing was perfect; she sang like a bird, without effort or artifice, for the sheer joy of singing. And when she stopped singing she pulled out a whistle from her blazer pocket and started to play that before anyone could draw breath. Then she sang again, two hauntingly lovely little songs . . . and then she simply stopped and smiled down from the platform at the audience. There was only a second of silence. Nobody could resist her. The applause was overwhelming. There were cries of "Bravo" and "Encore". We were even clapping in the wings. I didn't look round to see who was clapping and who wasn't or if anybody was checking me to see which I did. I just clapped till my palms stung.

Cora walked off the stage the other side. I saw Miss Todd bend to have a few words with her. Then Miss Todd walked on stage and held up a hand. "As you have obviously so much enjoyed the performance of our last pupil I have had a word with her and she is quite happy to provide a little encore." Crack! The applause went up again and on came Cora to sing two extra pieces. She was perfect. It dawned on me that these were songs of her mother's that she was singing. No wonder she had such grace and confidence out there; there was never any holding her given that inspiration.

The final performance of the choir was a bit of an anti-climax after that but nobody resented it. We were all rather proud that there had really been a show-stopper in the programme. It was strange, though—nobody mentioned Cora by name, neither fellow-pupils nor parents. People made remarks like: "Wasn't that last little soloist fantastic?" and "A real natural that folk-singer," and "That little dark-haired scrap stole the show, didn't she?" It was as if they couldn't quite bear to associate the singer who'd given them such rare pleasure with the child they'd virtually cast out from their midst.

In the car on the way home, however, Father, as usual, had no compunction about speaking his mind.

"I knew it from the start," he declared. "I took to that little Ravenwing girl right away. Real spark. Real originality. It's a disgrace the way she's been treated by everyone. I think someone should put a stop to it. Ask her to the house whenever you like, Becky."

"Oh, now, Edwin," said Mother cautiously. "Is that wise?"

"Be blowed to wisdom of that sort!" snorted Father. "That child is perfectly all right. More than that—she's got more talent than the rest of them put together." I felt momentarily deflated; perhaps I wasn't destined for the concert-hall after all.

"But, Edwin, just because a child can sing doesn't mean she's perfect in every other respect too. Remember Mrs. Briggs's tales . . . and certainly the other parents can't stand her."

"They applauded her roundly enough tonight."

"Indeed they did—but that just shows they're prepared to give praise where it's due. It doesn't necessarily mean they've changed their minds about her basically."

"Silly lot, then . . . We'll soon see what they think anyway . . ."

"Oh, Edwin! Promise you won't say a word. The whole evening will be ruined. And it'll be the second social disaster we've had on account of that little waif."

Mother and Father had been busy in the interval inviting the Fosters, Phillipses and Spensers back to the house for drinks. They'd asked Mrs. Briggs to set things out in the hopes of a little post-concert party and Mother was delighted that everyone was coming. As it happened, the gathering was great fun and nobody went home before half-past eleven. I didn't hear much of the adult conversation because we girls were bustled through to the kitchen, where Mrs. Briggs had left us a spread of sausages and crisps, but I did hear Father say to Mr. Phillips: "The Ravenwing child seems especially talented, don't you think?"

Mr. Phillips coughed loudly and looked at his wife. She said tartly: "Unfortunately a sweet voice doesn't mean a sweet child, does it?" and sipped her chilled white wine.

In the kitchen, Mrs. Briggs pulled on her bulky winter coat and knitted hat. "May I see the programme, dear? I like to see if there are any familiar names." She scanned it. "No, not this year. Don't know a soul."

"That was Cora Ravenwing, actually." I pointed to where it said: "Local Folk Music."

"Oh. Was it indeed!" she said. "I'm surprised she had the nerve. Silly of the school to put her on."

"She was the star of the whole thing."

"That one won't even be the star of her own funeral," she hissed and bundled herself out through the door.

"What did you say that for?" asked Susan.

"Because it's true."

Hermione, Barbara and Susan looked at me suspiciously.

Chapter 9 ❧ Fire

EVERYONE WAS FULL OF THE CONCERT NEXT DAY AT SCHOOL.
I saw several teachers stop to have a word with Cora in the
corridor but none of us said anything to her. I thought that
was particularly churlish. After Barbara and Susan and
Hermione and I had finished yet another round of clapping
each other on the back, I said: "Don't you think we should
tell Cora we thought she was good?"

"You must be joking!" said Susan.

"No, I'm not. Look at her, poor soul—the star of the
evening and nobody mentioning it."

Hermione gave me a stony look. "Why have you always
got to spoil things by bringing *her* in?"

"I'm not spoiling anything. What am I spoiling?"

"The fun we were having. We were all as cheerful as
anything and now you've messed it up." She flopped down
at her desk and got her things ready for the first lesson.

"She's right," said Barbara. "Why the constant loyalty
to Cora?"

"Oh, leave her alone," said Susan. "Forget the whole thing. You are a bit tiresome, though, Becky."

Then we all sat down grumpily, and fortunately Miss Turnbull came in and started in about how dismally bad we all were at arithmetic, so that, by the end of the lesson, we felt united again in our indignation against her and her slighting remarks about our intelligence. Barbara was the only one to feel smug, as she was specifically exempt from all the generalizations applied to the rest of us. I suppose that was only fair as she had gained ninety-four per cent in the last exam.

Nothing prevented me from congratulating Cora in the end. I managed to shove a note in her desk when nobody was looking. I said I thought hers had been the best item on the programme and could we meet as usual the next day, the last Thursday of term. Later, across the classroom, she gave me a quick nod.

When I met her in the cold, black, air-raid shelter she said: "I assumed we'd be meeting. You didn't need to risk up-setting your pals by communicating with me almost under their noses."

"Don't tease, Cora. I wanted to be sure we were going to meet, that's all. I shan't be able to over the Christmas holidays. I've had to lie about this evening. Everyone thinks it's very odd me having a piano lesson today when I've already had my quota for the term and the concert's over and everything. I've had to pretend I missed one earlier on."

"O.K. Keep your hair on. You're so earnest, Becky! What did you want to see me about so specially, anyway?"

"Just to tell you you were super at the concert," I said, feeling somehow that our earlier rôles were becoming more and more irrevocably reversed. The time had been when

Cora thought *I* was wonderful and trailed around after *me* in an irritatingly adulatory fashion. Now here was I doing the same to her. There was no doubt that I did admire her for the way she had coped with her lot: her mother-lessness, persecution by the spooky Mrs. Briggs, being out-cast by parents and pupils and so on. But what had finally clinched it was the superiority of her performance at the concert, my father's admiration for her, and her simple modesty.

"I enjoyed you and Barbara too."

"But you were so natural and unforced. It's all sort of *in* you without trying, whereas Barb and I worked on our duet for weeks."

"Oh, I worked on my whistle thing too."

"Still, you know what I mean. Were those songs by your mother?"

"Yes—words and music. I love them. Aren't they good? Better than Hermione's, don't you think?"

"I suppose they are. But then she was grown up. Her-mione's got years to improve."

"She won't improve. She'll only go off. Still, seeing you're being nice about me I won't start laying into your friend today! Did your parents like me?"

"Daddy did."

She looked pleased. I suspected she approved of him in the same way as he approved of her. "I like your dad."

"He spoke out in favour of you in front of other parents."

"I bet they didn't like that!"

"Not much!—And I showed Mrs. Briggs the programme too, and pointed out your thing and said it was you."

"Heavens! That was sticking your neck out. What did she say?"

"Not a lot! But she wasn't pleased."

"No—she wouldn't be, the old bat. Still, I'm glad you told her. It would be like a thorn in her flesh. I'd like to cram her flesh with thorns—the nasty old witch."

Cora had brought a little paraffin lamp into the air-raid shelter this time. It had a hollow green base which you filled with paraffin, and then there was a hole in the top to drop a wick in and screw it into place. She had lit the wick and dropped a little shade over the flame. It looked very pretty and gave more light than a candle. In her pleasure at the thought of Mrs. Briggs's vexation she threw out her arms and knocked the lamp over. At first nothing happened; the lamp went out and we fumbled about looking for it. Then I think Cora must have knocked over the bottle of paraffin she'd brought for refilling the lamp and then I knocked a candle over on top of that. Anyway, the spilt paraffin caught fire. Not much at first. We weren't frightened. "Oh, Becky, we're on fire," giggled Cora. "Put one of those rugs over it, quick!" I grabbed a rug. "Not that one," she said before I could do anything. "That's one of our decent ones." She scrambled around trying to pick out the shabbiest of our old blankets.

"Cora, get a move on!" I yelled. "It's spreading!"

Then there was the most almighty bang as the flames reached the paraffin bottle itself and flared up inside where a pool of paraffin was still trapped. Glass shot everywhere. Cora's face was caught in the sudden explosion of light, her eyes and mouth gaping, blood filling one eye. Flames and smoke were everywhere. The whole shelter was alight, a flaming tunnel from end to end. I couldn't see for smoke; I couldn't breathe for smoke; it curled round and round the arched roof; it was filling the place. And the entire floor seemed on fire. There was no escape. Cora's wiry hand grabbed mine. "Move!" she bellowed. I couldn't. She kicked my shins and pulled. *"Move!"* I don't know how we got to the ladder. My eyes were shut. But suddenly she jammed my hands on to a rung. "Climb!" I did, stumbling and choking up the rusty old rungs till my head came out among the clouds of smoke billowing into the field. Someone grabbed me and pulled me out into the darkening, damp evening. Then the face leaned down into the chimney again and the light from below flickered over the grim, streaked features of Mrs. Briggs, spluttering in the smoke.

"Cora's in there! Cora's in there!" I screamed through my own choking.

Her face leered down into the flames, a witch over her cauldron. "Is she indeed!" she cackled.

I leapt up and dashed to the side of the exit stack. "Cora!" I yelled. Then I could see her black head coming up towards us. "Cora! Quick!"

A huge fist plunged down into the shaft. A huge hand opened and spread over Cora's dark head, holding her down. Cora struggled; she turned her choking face up towards us; the hand spread over that too. Mrs. Briggs was pushing and grunting beside me, eyes closed as clouds of smoke gushed furiously up into her face. She was never going to let Cora out. With all my strength I rushed at her. I threw my entire body into her side and the impact bowled her over. She and I rolled down the grassy side of the air-raid shelter into the prickly, nettly grass at the bottom. I was up like a shot and scrambling back up the side in time to help Cora out at the top. She was wracked by coughs. I thought she'd choke to death but bit by bit she began to recover her breath. She clutched an exercise book under one arm. "I went back for this," she croaked. "I was going to show it to you." It was one of her mother's books.

Others had arrived in the field. They surrounded us now and helped us towards the gate. Mrs. Briggs was ahead of us on the arms of two farm men. Nobody asked us anything about how it had all happened; people were just gentle and kind. I remember soft murmurings of "Easy does it," and "All safe now". Only Mrs. Briggs's voice kept up an unearthly, shrieking monologue as we all struggled through the long grass. At the gate I turned and looked back at the shelter. Now flames were spurting out of both exits and two immense swelling balloons of thick white smoke were towering above in the evening sky. Someone said shakily: ". . . a narrow squeak! If it hadn't been for that woman . . ." I fainted—the first time in my life.

We were taken to the nearest house and an ambulance later took us and Mrs. Briggs to Heatherton Cottage Hospital. I don't remember it at all clearly now, but our lungs were checked and some bits of glass were removed from Cora's face and she had some stitches. Then we were sedated. I've no idea what was done with Mrs. Briggs. Some time later Mother and Father came and took me home. Cora was still sleeping when I left the ward. Her head was bandaged and she was just lying there motionless. Father wrapped me in a huge woolly blanket and carried me out. "Don't worry about your friend," a nurse whispered. "She's fine, but we're keeping an eye on her overnight. Her father has been already." At home Mother tucked me in my own bed and sat with me for a long time. Once she sobbed and said: "Oh . . . Becky!" But otherwise there was no comment on the incident.

In fact there was silence on the topic for at least a couple of days. Then it was almost Christmas; school holidays had started; Father had a few days off work. There were presents to buy, the tree to decorate, meals to plan and buy for. On

December the twenty-third, to the great joy of Jo and Dory, thick snow fell. They rushed out into the garden straight after breakfast to build igloos and snowmen. I was still at the table in my dressing-gown when there was a bumping and shuffling and shaking outside the back door, which then opened to admit the bulk of Mrs. Briggs coming in backwards. I'd completely forgotten it was her day and choked down my last piece of toast in an effort to get back upstairs before she saw me, but I was too slow. Panting and puffing clouds of steamy breath into the frosty air as she pulled her boots off and shook the snow on to the step, she addressed me over her shoulder. "None the worse then, dear?"

Mother intervened. "Becky's fine, Mrs. Briggs, and I'm glad to see you are too. I gather we've you to thank for the fact that the girls escaped at all." Mrs. Briggs grunted. "I came round to see you, actually," continued Mother. "But there was no reply. I didn't like to knock too long in case you were resting."

"I was," said Mrs. Briggs. "A shocking do! Fair took it out of me."

Father folded up his newspaper at the other end of the table. "I'm sure it was. I can't tell you how grateful we are, Mrs. Briggs. As a matter of fact we haven't begun to discuss the whole thing with Becky yet." He turned to Mother. "Why don't we all have a cup of coffee, dear, and sort it all out now?"

My heart turned over. Mrs. Briggs sat down heavily beside me. Mother made coffee in silence and set a mug in front of each of us.

"Well?" said Father, leaning his elbows on the table, cupping his chin in his hands and fixing me with a long stare.

"Oh, dear," I said desperately. "Is there any point going over it all? We're all safe, that's the main thing."

"Indeed it is," said Father firmly. "But we'll have your account if you don't mind. Then perhaps we can set our minds at rest that nothing like this is ever going to happen again. If it weren't for Mrs. Briggs, who risked her own life, it seems, you'd almost certainly have lost yours. So we'll just have the complete story right now. O.K.?" He continued to stare. Mother looked down into her coffee cup; I could see she was distressed. Mrs. Briggs, bright red from her walk through the snow, sniffed and sucked at her coffee.

There was no way of avoiding a row. "Cora and I had a den in the air-raid shelter," I admitted. "We used to meet there secretly once in a while—just for a few minutes. On Thursday she brought a paraffin lamp and we knocked it over and some paraffin got spilt and went up in flames."

"You realize you could both have been killed?" said Father icily. "Quite apart from the fact that you'd promised your Mother that you wouldn't have anything to do with Cora . . ."

"But you like her, Daddy. I thought as long as it was secret from everybody it wouldn't matter. And you yourself said after the concert . . ."

"Never mind what I said then," he interrupted. "Perhaps I was wrong. The fact remains that you were deceitful and the whole escapade was highly dangerous. If Mrs. Briggs . . ."

"She didn't do anything," I flashed. "We got out by ourselves. She didn't save us or anything like."

"Be quiet!" roared Father. "You've no recollection of what went on. I've heard eye-witness reports of how Mrs. Briggs pulled you out. She'd have pulled Cora out too only she was overcome by smoke. You wretched child! I'm ashamed!"

"Mrs. Briggs, I do apologize," mumbled Mother.

I couldn't say anything. The farm men must have misinterpreted what they saw as they struggled through the gloom, smoke and long grass to the shelter. And Mrs. Briggs must have spun such a yarn . . . How could I say that, far from saving Cora, she'd done her best to shove her back into the flames? And now she began to talk in such mild, wheedling, insinuating tones: "Mr. Stokes, Mrs. Stokes, please don't upset yourselves. I know kids. Becky's confused and upset, aren't you, dear? I know she doesn't remember what happened—perhaps it's for the best that she doesn't. I know she's not a bad girl. But I do beg you—and I'm afraid I'll have to repeat myself now—keep her away from that other one. She's *bad*. She's *rotten* through and through. She won't rest till she's killed someone. Mark my words, that's what'll happen. She seems driven to it. There's some that are mischievous and some that get themselves into all sorts of trouble they shouldn't—but there are some that are evil, black as the Devil himself, and she's one of those . . ."

"It's so hard to believe . . ." began Mother.

"We don't have to believe it," said Father, "though I'm almost beginning to. That sweet voice—bewitching—for good or evil? Who's to say?"

"Daddy!" I gasped. "Don't be daft! Cora's nice, and she's honest and good. Mrs. Briggs is lying. She's *mad*!"

"Go to your room," he thundered and leapt to his feet. He dragged my chair back from the table with me still sitting on it and my coffee slopped over the floor. I fled upstairs and locked myself in my bedroom.

Later he came up and tried the door. He shouted furiously. I didn't move and didn't speak. He hurled himself against the door, but it didn't give and after a while he went away. My knees were knocking with fright. I could hardly believe that my own father had filled me with such terror. I thought of Georgia Jamieson. I hardened against Father then; I don't think I every fully softened towards him again. I sat in my room all day. I saw Mrs. Briggs stumping off at noon. Sometimes the boys came running and whooping round the house, once pursued by Father tossing snowballs gently after them. I loved him and knew he was good and right in most ways, but I couldn't forgive him his total blindness earlier on and his fearsome raging at me.

In the evening, after the boys had been put to bed, there was a soft knock on my door and Mother called through: "Becky, I've brought you some tea. Do open up, dear. Daddy's gone to get cigarettes from the golf club; he won't be back for a bit." I let her in. Her face was blotched and swollen. "Becky, please patch this up with Daddy somehow. I don't care how you do it. But for all our sakes . . . What kind of a Christmas are we going to have at this rate?"

"I don't know if *he'll* patch it up with *me*. He's so furious."

"He's not so bad now. It was just so embarrassing you going for Mrs. Briggs like that after she'd practically killed herself saving you both."

My fists punched into the pillow beside me. "Mummy, she didn't, she *didn't*," I seethed. "She was just there, that's all. At most she gave me a hand at the top of the ladder, but Cora she tried to push down. I saw her. She had her hand on top of Cora's head. She wouldn't let her get out. And she didn't collapse because of the smoke. I shoved her out of the way. It was me—I pushed her down the side of

the air-raid shelter so Cora could get out. She tried to mur-
der her."

Mother sat down, white and shocked. She believed me,
I thought. "Oh, Becky! What are we going to do with you?
What's got into you? How can you say such things . . .?"

My heart sank. "Go away," I whispered. "What's the
use? Nobody believes me." She went out silently. I sobbed
desperately. I longed to see Cora. She knew the truth. I
didn't even know if she was home from hospital.

Much later, after I'd tucked myself in bed—I'd never got
out of my pyjamas all day—Mother and Father came to
see me together. They were sad and grave but determined
to mend matters. I had wept for hours and felt very tired;
the intensity of my hurt feelings and my sense of injustice
and outrage had dulled. I could understand how they had
been tricked by Mrs. Briggs. They weren't so unusual in
that; she had the entire village under her thumb. Father
took my hand and stroked it as I lay there. He spoke for
both of them. "Let's draw a curtain over this entire episode,
Becky. We're all upset. We're never going to see eye to
eye. You believe your version and we believe ours. Maybe
you're still shocked; maybe you'll never have a clear recollection of what happened. Let's leave it at that."

"O.K.," I agreed quietly. "How's Cora? Do you know?"

"Your mother phoned this morning. She's home and she's
well. Just shocked, like you. But Mother and I have decided,
and Mr. Ravenwing agrees, that there's no good being
served by this secret friendship between you and Cora—so
it's got to stop. I do, now, definitely forbid you to have any
dealings whatsoever with that child. I think we've all learned
our lesson now. What do you say?"

"All right."

I wasn't going to argue. At least they hadn't made me

promise. I would keep the peace and Christmas would go ahead in its usual jolly way. But I had no intention at all of keeping away from Cora. We would simply have to bide our time. That was all. The tie that bound us was stronger than ever. I was sure she must feel that too.

Chapter 10 ❧ Footprints in the Snow

IT'S SURPRISING HOW THE MOST DEVASTATING OF FAMILY rows can, to all intents and purposes, blow over in a flash. Christmas day was as noisy as ever in our house, with presents, and phone calls from relatives, and church, and turkey. Now and then I would recall Father's rage and Mother's woe of two days earlier but both seemed unreal in the light of family carol-singing and party hats. And after Christmas was over it wasn't so long until the new term started.

I was dreading seeing Hermione and Susan and Barbara again. I hadn't had a letter or a phone call from any of them over the holidays and wondered why not. Inevitably Mrs. Briggs would have broadcast her version of events at the air-raid shelter but, even if they were angry about my secret liaison with Cora, I was surprised that they weren't worried about how I was. Heavens! If one of them had come that close to death I'd have been round in a trice.

I met Hermione on the way to school on the first day of term.

She said: "Hello. Are you all right now?"

"Fine. I was all right all along, really."

We walked on in silence for a bit.

"I'm sorry I didn't come and see you, Becky."

"I was hoping you would."

"Mummy and Daddy weren't keen. They said it'd be better to let you get everything sorted out with your parents."

"*What* sorted out?"

"Well, about Cora and everything."

"Oh, I see. Yes, I suppose that all got sorted out."

"Why did you do it, Becky?"

"Oh, I don't know. At the beginning it was really that I thought it would be terribly mean to leave her high and dry after I'd been so friendly with her all summer. And then, later, I began to enjoy meeting her."

There was another painful silence.

"Who's your real best friend, Becky? Me or Cora?"

I didn't know what to say. "Oh . . . it's hard . . . you're both so different."

Hermione said sadly: "You'll have to decide, you know. You've been awfully deceitful—worse than Horti with Hector, and that was bad enough. I never lied to you or kept secrets you didn't know about. If you really promised me you'd never let me down again I might be able to forgive you and things might be as nice again as they used to be, but I'm not certain. I would try. But you'd really have to swear on the Bible."

I was stuck. I would never be overtly friendly with Cora, that was certain. Mother and Father wouldn't allow that. How could I forego all other friendships as well? I loved to have friends. I couldn't imagine myself as another Georgia or Cora. I cast desperately around in my mind for some formula to cover the demands of the situation. It mustn't be a lie but it couldn't quite be all the truth either. Hermione was waiting.

I said: "Mummy and Daddy have forbidden me to have anything to do with Cora."

"Didn't they do that before?"

"No, not really. They were in two minds. Daddy quite liked her at one stage, I think. But anyway they've definitely both decided against her now."

"And how about you?"

I hesitated.

She burst out: "How can you be in any doubt? She tried to kill you, didn't she? Mrs. Briggs said if she hadn't been cleaning at the school and coming home at precisely that moment you'd have been done for."

Through clenched teeth I said: "Whatever else we discuss let's leave Mrs. Briggs right out of it, shall we? I hate her."

"But she saved . . ."

"She did not save either of us. *Please* . . ."

Hermione was puzzled and hurt by my manner, but I couldn't help it. Just as she was making demands of me in the name of past friendship so I had to make them of her. In the end, when we met up with Barbara and Susan, I had to promise faithfully never to have anything to do with Cora again. None of them would settle for less. I made my false promise but felt alienated from them all for pushing me into it. I knew I would never keep it. As the term got under way we all pretended that things were as they had always been, but I don't think I was alone in knowing that they weren't. We still had fun at school and visited each

others' houses, but they each had an underlying deep suspicion of me. Sometimes, during a lull in conversation, I
would suddenly be aware of a strange stillness and I would
look up and find myself gazing into three pairs of unblinking eyes. They were on the watch.

Thick snow continued to lie over Okefield for most of
January, and finally even Jo and Dory became sick of it as
Mother grew more and more bad-tempered about puddles
and wet footmarks all over the kitchen floor. One morning,
while we were all gulping down our cereal before school,
Father came in with the milk bottles, looking a bit troubled.
"Come and look at this, Jean," he said.

"What! Right now?" said Mother, peering under the
grill to check toast.

Father nodded crossly.

"What's going on?" I asked.

"There you are," said Father to Mother. "Now everybody's wanting to know. Sit down, Jo. There's nothing to
see. And just you stay put too, Becky, and get on with your
breakfast."

They went out through the front door. After a while I
sneaked into the hall and peeped out to see what they were
doing. They seemed to be aimlessly tramping round in the
front garden, looking hard on the ground and then up at
my bedroom window. When they showed signs of being
about to come in again I shot back into the kitchen unobserved.

"All right?" I asked casually.

"Did you hear anything unusual last night, Becky?" said
Father.

"No. Why? What's out there? What have you seen?"

"It's nothing, dear," said Mother quickly. "There's bound

to be a simple explanation. Perhaps the milkman was looking for one of us to pay the bill or something."

"Not the same boots," said Father. "I thought of that one already. The milkman's footmarks are quite different."

"Footmarks? What footmarks?"

"There are some strange boot-marks in the snow at the front of the house," said Father. "They just go along close to the wall—they don't seem to be going anywhere, really."

"A burglar, do you think?" I felt quite frightened.

"I can't really believe it—we've nothing worth stealing but . . ."

When I was ready for school they let me examine the footmarks too. They could see I was alarmed in any case. They were distinct, deep imprints in the snow, and they went right along the front of the house and came to a halt under my bedroom window. There the "burglar" appeared to have paused for a moment or two, making quite a muddle of prints before retracing his steps and leaving by the front gate.

"Strange, isn't it?" said Father. "Big feet but small steps. Did you notice? Don't worry, darling. He seems to have thought better of it anyway."

"Won't you get the police?" I said. "What if he comes back?"

"Most unlikely," said Father. "No, I think I'll just leave it. But we'll keep our eyes open for a day or two, shall we?"

I certainly did that. I hardly got a continuous hour of sleep for the next three nights. I was constantly starting awake, hearing things, seeing shadows, steeling myself to sit up in bed and peer through a chink in the curtains. There was never anyone there. On the fourth night I slept very deeply and bounced down for breakfast feeling much happier, only to be confronted by Father, all grey and worried, in the hall, saying: "I'm getting the police in this time, Jean." Mother agreed and he phoned then and there. The same footprints were outside in the snow again, treading out the same track along the front of the house and coming to a standstill under my bedroom window. I felt very unnerved. But at least the police were coming; that would be exciting. Perhaps it'd be the same man who came making enquiries after the air-raid shelter fire. He had been very understanding then and I felt comforted to think he might be in charge of this case. Nobody had come before it was time for school, though. "Same old story," grumbled Father. "Nobody around when they're needed. The snow'll be melted before they get here." He roared off to the station in the car and Mother was left to handle things.

At school I made a melodramatic tale out of the situation and gathered a crowd round me. In the background I was aware of Cora's face turned in my direction. I hadn't spoken to her all term, nor had we dared to exchange secret notes, but often our eyes would meet and I never doubted that she, like myself, was only waiting for the chance to carry on where we'd left off. And this time our secrecy would have to be foolproof.

"Imagine!" exclaimed Susan. "The police again! They're never out of your house these days, Becky. You'll be getting a frightful record!"

"Don't be silly. You've got to have done something wrong for that. Last time they just decided to let the matter rest, and this time I'm definitely the injured party."

"Do you think there's someone after you?" said Hermione. "Have you seen anyone lurking about or following you or anything?"

"No, I don't, and no, I haven't!" I said. "Are you trying to frighten me to death?"

"No, but you've got to be careful. Mummy says there are funny men on the common."

"Oh, I know she does. Mummy won't let me go any more. But I used to go quite a lot and I never saw anyone."

Barbara could see a quarrel brewing. She said: "Who do you think it is, then?"

"Well—a burglar. I suppose."

"But why stop outside *your* window?"

"I don't know. That's odd. It give me the creeps, actually. Maybe the drainpipe down the wall there looks easier than all the others."

"That's a bit feeble."

"Oh, well," I blustered, "if he comes again tonight and carries me off I'll be able to put you all in the picture, won't I?"

"Don't say such things, even as a joke, Becky," said Hermione, all shocked. I was mean enough to think that she wasn't really scared about the possibility of anything happening to me, only in so far as if it could happen to me it could happen to her too. I had begun to see her through Cora's eyes.

The man didn't come that night, anyway. In fact he never came back. For the first week or two the police agreed to patrol our area more frequently than usual during the hours of darkness but, bit by bit, their vigilance slackened off and the snow melted and we moved into spring. Everyone seemed happier the warmer it became and by the end of April there was a general air of relaxation throughout the village. Doors were left open, people dawdled over shopping and strolled around enjoying the sunshine and blossom. It was the moment Cora and I had been waiting for. One Saturday morning, as I came out of Copcutt's, having spent my pocket-money on a stack of cheap sweets, I ran straight into her on the way in. She hurriedly stepped out again and muttered: "I'll run back up to the church and wait for you." Then she ran off.

I hung around Copcutt's window for a few minutes, chewing sweets in the sun, and then I set off after her. On the way I met Barbara and Derek on bikes. They stopped and talked for about a quarter of an hour, and all that time I tingled with the excitement of knowing I had an assignation with Cora which they and their like had done all in their power to prevent. I smiled and chatted and shared my sweets and was the model friend. I felt no guilt towards them at all. If I was dishonourable in breaking my promise, then Barbara and the others had been equally at fault in forcing me into it in the first place. At last they cycled off, cheerful and freckly and unsuspecting, and I made my way casually up the lane to the church. I was expecting Cora to be at her mother's graveside as usual, but when I got there she was nowhere in sight.

"Psst! Becky!" I turned, and there she was, beckoning me from a little door at the bottom of the church tower.

"Good heavens, Cora! What are you doing there?" I hurried over and stepped inside. She pulled the door shut.

"Come upstairs," she said. "Follow me. Don't be scared." She started up the stone spiral stairs which I guessed must go round and round inside the tower right up to the belfry. I went up behind her. We didn't speak. The scraping of our feet echoed up and down the tower and we were soon panting with the effort of the climb.

At last we came out on to a wooden platform. I flopped on the floor in a heap and looked round. Above us hung a huge black bell, its clapper dangling motionless. "Good grief!" I gasped. "Does that thing ring?"

Cora laughed. "No, that's never used. The clock chimes come from somewhere else."

"Thank heaven for that! Big bells like that can drive you mad, you know, if they start up right in your ears."

"Oh, relax, Becky! Don't you think this is a marvellous place for us to meet?"

"What's that great mess over there?" I asked, indicating a huge heap of sticks, rags and paper which someone seemed to have gone to enormous lengths to carry up.

"It's a nest, silly."

"A nest!"

"Yes. Jackdaws. There's a little nesty bit in the middle at the top, all soft and lined with rags and feathers."

"Any eggs?"

"Not yet. Should be any day."

"Doesn't anyone ever come up here?"

"I've never seen anyone. Dad does, now and then, just to check the tower's not actually falling down. But hardly ever. We're safe as houses up here."

I began to feel safe. "How've you been, Cora? It's super to see you again. I knew we would, didn't you? Have you been forbidden to speak to me?—I'm not allowed near you."

"Mmmm. Dad said your parents had been pretty adamant about that and he wasn't bothered. He just told me that he and I were a pair of misfits and I'd find life easier if I took that in once and for all and stopped trying to have friends."

"What did he say about the fire? Was he scared about what might have happened?"

"Not really. I told him there was never really any chance of us getting killed."

"Oh, Cora! There was! Don't you think so?"

She looked at me, surprised. "No, there wasn't, Becky. You just panicked a bit, that's all. I could see the way out all the time. I only got a bit burned because I went back for Mum's book."

"Well, Mrs. Briggs told everyone we were done for and she saved us . . ."

"Tommy rot!"

"I know! I know very well she didn't save us—but I suppose I took her word for the rest of it. I really thought we'd been at death's door."

"Well, I suppose people can die in the silliest of accidents if they lose their heads. But not us! I tell you one thing, though . . ."

"What?"

"I don't know whether you saw this or not, but Mrs. Briggs seemed to be pushing me back down again. I was just getting to the top of the ladder when I felt this great pushing and shoving against the top of my head. And I looked up and there was this old hag leaning in trying to hold me down. That's what I thought. Then suddenly she disappeared . . ."

"It's true, Cora. It *is* true. I was there by the ladder and I saw her. I've tried to tell Mummy and Daddy but they won't believe me."

"Might as well save your breath as speak out against Mrs. Briggs."

"But she didn't disappear—I shoved her out of the way to give you a chance to get out."

Cora looked at me for a long time. "Did you really, Becky? Then it was you who saved me. I think she was really going to do me in that time. I wasn't sure, but if *you* think . . ."

"Well, I definitely thought so."

In the silence that followed as Cora absorbed that shocking fact there was a sudden fluttering and scrabbling about on the other side of the loft. I thought someone was coming and leapt up guiltily, heart thumping.

Cora laughed. "Relax, you ass! It's Whacky."

"Who's Whacky?"

She just pointed across the floor and there was a jackdaw strutting fussily towards the nest with a bright pink rag in its beak. Its claws rattled on the planking. Cora held out a hand and the jackdaw cocked its grey-capped head on one side and peered at her out of one cool, pearl-grey eye. I'd never been so near a wild bird before.

"Tchacka, tchacka, tchack," it squawked loudly.

"She's O.K., Whacky. A real friend," said Cora and the bird came over and jumped on to her hand. She lifted him up to her face and talked away to him as if he understood every word. She looked like a bird herself, jabbing and jutting her sharp little nose at him while she spoke and staring into his bright grey eyes with her shiny black ones. When he'd had enough he jumped down and flapped up on top of the great pile of junk that was his nest. He was lost to view, but we could hear him scratching and poking away amongst the twigs. "He'll be fixing that bit of pink rag in the nest."

"Will his mate come along soon?"

"She might. I know her too. They've nested here for years. They just patch up the old nest and re-use it. There's a rookery out in the churchyard—have you seen it? Sometimes they hang around with the rooks out there. And often they go off and forage in the fields with them."

I was impressed by her knowledge. "Golly! You know a lot about them."

"That's what happens when you've no friends. You've got to fill up your time somehow—so I spend ages outside, watching animals and things."

"You're a funny girl, Cora. There's lots more to you than anyone knows about."

"Whose fault's that?" She shrugged. "Never mind. It's enough for me that you're beginning to know me." She caught my sleeve suddenly. "Tell you what!"

"What?"

"I could show you loads of animals and things you've never seen if you come out at night with me."

"*Night!*"

"Yes. I often go out on the common at night."

"But, Cora, it's dangerous. There are men hanging around there at night. Nobody's allowed there—I'm not even allowed to go during the day."

"That's all rubbish. I've never seen anybody. Well—a few couples kissing and things, but I just steer clear of them and they're definitely not interested in me. They never see me anyway. One thing about watching animals—you learn to be ever so quiet."

"I couldn't come, Cora. I'd be scared stiff in the dark—and Mummy and Daddy'd be livid if they found out."

"Just a thought . . . Actually I came for you once or twice soon after Christmas. I threw snow up at your window but you didn't hear me. You must sleep like a log."

"Good grief! You've got a nerve, Cora. We're not supposed even to be speaking to each other and yet you come creeping around at dead of night! What if Daddy'd seen you?"

"I tell you, I'm never seen if I don't want to be. You'd be safe with me, Becky. At least think about it. It'd be much more exciting than meeting up here once in a while."

Something was vaguely falling into place in my mind. "Cora," I said slowly. "Were those *your* footmarks outside our house—the ones that Daddy eventually got the police to look at?"

She laughed. "Must've been. I thought that when I heard you telling everyone at school about your burglar. Good thing you *did* make a great story out of it or I might have come again and been set on by police!"

"But what on earth had you got on your feet? They were massive great footprints."

"Dad's wellingtons. Mine had got a hole in and I just came out in his. Just as well—it was enough to put you all off the scent."

I was amused and relieved to think that, after all, it had been little Cora and not some grim maniac hanging around the house. And I began to think again about the common —perhaps it wasn't peopled after dark by madmen after all. I wanted to tell Cora I'd go with her on one of her night-time jaunts but I wasn't sure I dared. Instead, almost for pratice, I inveigled Hermione into playing truant with me. This was when we made off together to commune with nature instead of going to school. It was a marvellous day but all the time I was disloyally aware of the shortcomings of my companion. Not only was she as ignorant of the ways of the countryside as I was but she didn't really seem interested in nature itself, only in so far as she could use it to influence her mood and thoughts and thereby work up some poem or other. She didn't really examine it for its own sake—she just went on examining herself through it; her reactions to it were what concerned her. I'd found her so fascinating at first. Now I began to be actually bored by her self-absorption. It was now, too, that my special trio of friends pushed me into betraying Cora by participating with them in their "curse". I never told Cora how I'd stuck thorns into her effigy, much as she'd once declared she'd like to ram them into Mrs. Briggs, and I never took the curse seriously. Bit by bit, my loyalties changed.

Meanwhile, schooldays rolled on happily enough with friendships continuing as established at the beginning of the year. It would have been far too inconvenient and disruptive if people had started questioning whether they really, in fact, *liked* their "friends". Everybody knew who was whose friend and that was that.

I loved the summer term. The weather was warm again and we all wore short socks and sandals and gingham dresses. Some teachers let us sit out of doors for lessons, and there were treats like rounders and practising for sports day and Miss Tidmarsh, who took us for nature-study, lining us up in a crocodile for rambles. Once she took all seventeen of us on the common and we were late back for lunch, and we heard she got quite a row from Miss Todd. Actually, that walk on the common was just about what did it—that, plus the taste for adventure that I got when I went that day with Hermione. By mid-May I was thoroughly determined to go with Cora on a night-time expedition. We made our arrangements in the bell-tower during one of our infrequent, clandestine meetings there. She would come for me the first fine night and take me off to experience, at first hand, sights and sounds of nature that I'd only hitherto read about.

Chapter 11 ❧ Night Freedom

THE ONLY DIFFICULTY WE FORESAW WAS WAKING ME UP IN the first place. I was indeed a heavy sleeper. We hit on the bizarre solution that I should tie one end of a reel of cotton round my little finger and then drop the whole reel out of the window. My bed ran alongside the window and I could easily leave the sash slightly open all night. If Cora came she would look for the reel on the flower-bed under my window and pull on it to wake me. If she didn't I could snap the thread in the morning, drop the loose end out, and retrieve the whole lot and rewind it later in the day. I was sure that if Mother found it before me she would only conclude that one of the boys had been messing around with it—she'd never dream it was part of an elaborate conspiracy between Cora and me. In fact, it wasn't all that marvellous an idea. Several times I snapped the cotton by mistake as I rolled over in my sleep and I wouldn't have felt a thing if Cora had come on one of those nights. But, as it happened, it was still intact the first night she actually did come.

I awoke to the oddest little twitching sensation in my finger. It seemed to be jerking all by itself. Then I realized it was being tugged. It reminded me of the tiny, bobbing, nibbling pulls I'd felt when fishing for flounders from a rowing boat one summer. I lay in a semi-dream, remembering the thrill of getting a bite, when suddenly a slightly sharper jerk brought me right round with a jump. Cora! I leapt up in bed and peered out into the dark. There she was, remarkably clear in the moonlight, cupping her hands round her mouth and whispering, "Hurry up, for heaven's sake!" I snapped the cotton and dropped it out, then I pulled the curtain across again and switched on my bedside lamp. I threw on the first clothes that came to hand and tiptoed downstairs, holding my breath. As I grabbed my mac in the hall the belt buckle swung out and banged loudly against the wall. I thought the game was up and stood transfixed, waiting for lights to go on and Father to appear at the top of the stairs. But nothing happened. I sneaked through to the kitchen—it was one-thirty by the clock there—and let myself out of the back door. At the front of the house Cora and I confronted one another with glee. "Come on!" she whispered and snatched my hand. "Let's clear off!" We ran lightly across the lawn, out through the gate, and off up the road in the direction of the common.

Cora had everything planned, it seemed. Once beyond our garden hedge we stopped running and walked quietly up through the village. Our sandals made no sound; we seemed to glide over the pavement. Everywhere was still and dark; house and street lights were all out; Copcutt's on the corner was black as pitch. We held hands tightly and spoke in whispers, though at first I was too excited for words at all. The air was mild and warm and, now and then, heavily scented—we would walk through a sudden wave of perfume, then turn to see where it came from and discover thick apple-blossom or a border of wall-flowers in someone's garden. As we made our way up the road towards Cora's house and the church, the hedges closed in on either side of us and made it darker than before. My heart began to pound as I realized that we'd have to pass the field with the air-raid shelters and the graveyard. But Cora babbled in my ear and hardly gave my imagination a chance to sweep me off into fearful fantasies.

"It was easy, wasn't it, Becky? See, you can do anything you want now. We can go out ever so many nights, see each other for hours. What do you think of night? Have you ever been out so late before? It seems still, doesn't it? But just you wait—the common's more alive at night than during the day!"

At that point there was a fantastic, ear-splitting shriek right over our heads and something swept by, giving us about an inch of clearance. I felt the draught as it swooped past. "Cora!" I screamed, and clutched her in panic.

"Screech owl—there're loads round here."

I recovered almost at once, unburied my face from her shoulder, and looked about for it—much too late, of course. "I've never seen one. Blast! I've missed it."

"We may see it again up at the church."

When we got there Cora made to go through the gate. "Oh, I don't know," I said, hanging back.

"Come on!" she said firmly, pulling me by the arm. "You've got to come up and see Whacky and mate. They've hatched out five chicks, you know."

"Won't it put them out if we go clattering up?"

"That's a feeble excuse," she said and her grinning teeth caught the moonlight. She looked like a skull!

I leaned feebly against the gate. "I can't, Cora. I'm petrified!"

But somehow she yanked me in round the gate and we crunched up the path round the back of the church and shoved open the bell-tower door. It was pitch black in there but, before I could protest, Cora switched on a little torch to light us up the steps. There was a lot of flapping and tchack-tchacking as we approached the top, but Cora called up to the jackdaws that it was only us and by the time we arrived all was peaceful. "Let me show Becky your chicks, Whacky," whispered Cora. "They're so beautiful."

Whacky flapped down from the heap of sticks and strutted proudly back and forth. I could see another jackdaw's head sticking out at the top. "That's the female," said Cora. "She'll shift in a minute if I give her some food and then you'll be able to see the chicks. Here, you hold the torch and stand on tiptoe." She pulled a screw of paper from her pocket and emptied it into her hand. "Here, girl, corn," she said, and the greedy female struggled up off her chicks at once and climbed down on to Cora's wrist. I stretched my arm up as far as I could, stood on tiptoe and directed the slender beam of torch-light into the nest. Sure enough, five ugly, bristly, little heads popped up on long wobbly necks. As I craned forward I nearly overbalanced on to the pile of twigs. "Watch out!" hissed Cora. I felt abashed and shone the torch on her. She was sitting on the floor with the jackdaws beside her, eating from her hand. "Greedy pair, aren't they?" she said smiling up at me. The sharpness in her voice had been only a warning-note.

I was to hear it often during our night outings, as she jerked me back from a rabbit-hole I was about to stick my foot in, or stopped me from blundering straight into a concealed pool. Her eyes were as sharp as a cat's, her sense of smell like a fox's. I stumbled blindly after her and would have scarcely seen anything if she hadn't shown me.

Later, that first night, we went on the common. By this time I was finding it quite a strain trying to see. I felt as if my eyes were reaching right out of their sockets in an effort to make the most of the moonlight.

"Are we going to see anything special? Or are we just here on the off-chance?" I whispered.

"You can speak normally, you know. There's nobody around."

But I couldn't speak normally. I jumped and trembled at every crackle underfoot or puff of wind and hung on to Cora's arm as if my life depended upon it. What I thought she could possibly do in the event of any of my worst horrors actually materialising I've no idea. But at least I was determined not to lose her. We ended up in a little wood on one side of the common. I'd never been here before. It was very dark; the leaves rustled and hushed, rustled and hushed, as the breeze came and went. I wasn't sorry when Cora sat down with her back to a big tree-trunk and pulled me down beside her.

"Let's sit here for a bit and see what happens," she said and pulled out a bag of toffees. "Try not to make a row chewing and rattling papers."

"What might happen?"

"You'll see. Don't talk."

We sat for a long time, hunched together, silent. At one stage my eyes stopped bulging and popping out of my head and nearly closed instead. Sleep was amazingly near. Then Cora nudged me and I could hear a grunting, snuffling, snorting very close by. It seemed to be right beside us and I snatched my feet up under me. "Shh!" hissed Cora in my ear. Suddenly she switched on a little red light and in its glow I made out a black-and-white striped badger-head some yards off—further away than I'd thought. It was poking up out of a hole, nose in the air, sniffing and peering. Then out it came, about three feet of it in all, like a hunched-up, hairy, grey dog, and began grubbing about along a little pathway outside its hole. I knew of the existence of badgers, of course, but the sight of it there, right under my nose, shook me.

I brought my lips right up to Cora's ear. "Will it attack us?"

She didn't speak but I saw her shaking her head and smiling.

"They can't see this red light," she whispered later. "It used to belong to Mum, you know." Then she pointed and I looked back at the hole to see another badger-head popping out—a baby one—followed by two more. These were much less cautious than the adult as they burst out of the confines of the sett, and rolled and romped around on the sandy path and in and out of the bracken on either side. The air was full of their grunts and whimpers and squeals and snorts. The adult largely ignored them and busied itself rolling up bundles of bracken and shuffling backwards into its tunnel with the whole lot under its chin. I was thoroughly engrossed in watching all the antics and totally relaxed for the first time since I'd crept out of the house. Then suddenly a blood-curdling scream from somewhere deeper in the wood came ripping through the air. It sounded as if someone was being slaughtered. I gaped at Cora but, before I could speak, two more screams tore through the darkness. The badgers stood stock-still, noses in the air.

"Switch the torch off—we'll be seen!" I tried to grab the torch from Cora.

"Shut up, you idiot!" she snapped. "It's another badger."

"*That!* It *can't* be! *Please* put the light out."

"We won't see it if I do."

"That was a *human* scream. There *is* someone there. Something awful's happening. Let's run for it." My temples were throbbing with terror. I stood up.

Then: "Look! Look!" said Cora and pointed. Another big badger came nosing along the path towards the sett. He sniffed at the others and pushed his way past them into the hole. With one accord they all followed and, in no time, there we were again, just Cora and me, alone, with our backs against a tree-trunk, in the middle of a wood, in the middle of the night.

"Sorry," I said.

"That's O.K.," she said. "Have another toffee. Then we should go, I think."

All the way home she told me details about badgers and their ways, and I wasn't frightened at all. I crept in our back door at half-past four, locked it behind me and sneaked upstairs to bed. Nobody heard me.

In the morning I didn't know whether to feel very clever or very guilty as Mother bustled round making breakfast and the usual good-humoured conversation. Her cheerfulness made me irritable but at school, as I day-dreamed sleepily through the lessons and gazed at the back of Cora's black head, the thrills of our night excursion rushed back to me. I couldn't wait to go again.

And we did go. Lots of times. They were nights I have never forgotten—usually warm, and still, and starlit, but sometimes Cora would come on a night that was windy and wild, and we'd watch the branches bowing and clouds tossing across the face of the moon. Cora usually had something specific in mind for us to watch or hear, but not always. We heard nightingales and nightjars and owls. We watched the badgers on numerous occasions and saw bats and once a fox. One night we went to the big pond on the common and listened to the croak-croaking of vast numbers of frogs. If it rained we went into the bell-tower and sheltered with Whacky. Once we sat up there in a thunderstorm and heard the huge black bell overhead reverberating echoes of the thunder peals and saw each other's faces as clear as day in the flashes of lightning which shot in through invisible cracks in the stonework. Sometimes we sat in Cora's garden-shed and talked, and played with her pet hedgehog, Thatch. At first I used to feel a bit sick watching him guzzle down the worms and slugs we took him, but in the end I fell for him, prickles, ticks and all. We very seldom saw anybody at all during our escapades; odd rustles and thumps would turn out to be birds and rabbits we'd disturbed. Occasionally we'd almost stumble over a courting couple but, as Cora had predicted, they didn't have eyes for us. Only on one occasion did anything unusual or spine-chilling happen.

It was a gusty, blustery, black sort of night. At times the wind would clear the moon for a few seconds and an eerie, silver light would shimmer on ruffled puddles and our wet faces. Then it would be black as pitch again for half an hour or so. We were bumping against each other as we stumbled across the common and laughing a bit hysterically and thinking of Robert Louis Stevenson's galloping horseman. Cora was teasing me, I remember, and I was giggling nervously. "Whenever the trees are crying aloud," she was intoning in the complete blackness . . . When, suddenly, the moon shone out again—and there was a bulky, black-cloaked figure right in our path. We all saw each other at once as the moon shone full on our startled, grey-white, night faces. The figure straightened up and pushed back its dripping hair—its lips were black and gaping, its nose hooked, its eyes wild. It was Mrs. Briggs.

I couldn't move.

Cora seized my hand. She screamed once: "Run!" The moon went out and we turned in the dark and dashed for it. Cora was fleet and sure-footed. Without her I would have fallen flat on my face in seconds. For a while we could hear the cursing Mrs. Briggs plunging after us. But at last we were sure we had left her far behind and that the panting and puffing we fancied we heard when we stopped dead to listen was only the wind which we'd been enjoying so much earlier.

"D'you think she knew it was us?" I gasped.

Cora looked at me closely in the torchlight as we squatted in the shed beside a rummaging Thatch. We both had macs on with hoods pulled up and tied tightly under our chins. "Not for sure. You don't look like you with your hair all pushed back under your hood. And she only caught a glimpse of us."

"I knew it was her, though—instantly!"

"Oh, well—she's unmistakable!"

"What on earth was she doing out on the common by herself on a night like this?"

"Exactly!"

"What a sight she was! She really looked like a witch, didn't she?"

"I'm always telling you."

"Oh, but there aren't such things . . ."

"Well, you just think on. That's all I say. I'm prepared to call a witch a witch even if you're not."

We sat in silence for a while and I considered the matter. At last I said: "Nonsense, Cora! You're entitled to think the worst of her after what she's put you through—but I don't see how she can possibly be a witch! I *know* they don't exist. I bet she'd been babysitting over on the estate. The Spensers have her regularly—I know that for a fact—and probably loads of other people do as well." But Cora just snorted and I knew she would persist in her own spooky beliefs whatever I said.

Later, when the rain stopped, we scurried back to my house. Cora came with me; she always did, and then went back home alone. I knew it was unfair, but I couldn't have steeled myself to come out at all if I'd had to be alone in the dark for even the shortest time. I was always totally dependent on Cora during the night, but she never made me feel small. We were both a bit alarmed at the possibility that Mrs. Briggs had recognized us and might tell my parents, so we didn't go out for about a week. But when nothing was said or heard we concluded that she hadn't known it was us and resumed as before.

By the end of June the late nights were beginning to tell on me. I was used to feeling tired and was no longer irritable, but I had become permanently dreamy and light-headed in a way which was noticeable both at home and at school. At first that had the effect of making everyone else irritable, but eventually Mother became more worried than cross and took me off to Doctor Fairhurst. He couldn't find anything wrong with me, of course, which was a great relief to Mother, but, all the same, I felt that she was becoming extra watchful over me at that time and I decided that Cora and I had better take a break for a bit and let me get thoroughly rested. I would tell her the next time she came.

As it happened, she came that very night. After the visit to the doctor I'd gone up for an early night. He'd told Mother I was probably just finding life a bit demanding with puberty coming on. "Nothing a bit more sleep won't cure," he'd said, all jovial. Mother had been especially gentle on the way home and embarrassed us both by talking about all the little changes I could expect to find going on in myself now I was on the verge of womanhood. I had squirmed around hotly and stumbled on and off the kerb to cover my self-consciousness. I had been glad when we arrived home and Jo and Dory put a stop to the possibility of all such intimate discussion. I went to bed about half-past eight and was very deeply unconscious when the finger-jerking started up about one o'clock. As I came to fully, waved to Cora, and dropped my end of the cotton through the window, I heard the sounds of someone in the bathroom. Mother and Father must only just have come up to bed. I waited some minutes before dressing cautiously and tiptoe-ing out on to the landing. I could see a strip of light under their door; they must be reading. I hesitated momentarily, wondering whether to retreat, and then, on impulse, scurried on down the stairs, across the hall and kitchen and out through the back door.

"Get going!" I said, racing past Cora to the gate. "They're still awake!"

"Did they see you?" she panted behind me, in some alarm.

"Course not, you ass! I'd hardly be here if they had!"

Soon we were well on our way to the common, scarcely able to stifle our mirth at imagined conversations between my parents and me supposing they *had* seen me. "Oh, off for a night on the common with Cora? How nice, dear! Don't hurry back. Make the best of the weather. Got sandwiches?" I said in Mother's voice, and Cora spluttered and screeched and held her ribs.

We decided to go and watch badgers again, because I

felt sleepy and thought it might be quite nice to drop off now and then and leave it to Cora to nudge me if they appeared. I explained to her how tired I'd been getting and that we'd better have a week or two's break and she agreed.

"You poor old thing," she said softly. "Need your sleep, do you? I can go on for ever with scarcely any."

"Maybe you can. It's just another of the ways in which you're totally anti-social, then. Who'd ever want to live with someone who didn't need any sleep?"

"Someone else who doesn't need any sleep. Not that it needs to make much difference to anybody else—I'm very quiet," she said, all prickly.

I yawned. "I'm only joking, Cora," I said, giving her a mild poke, and she took my arm and smiled and said she knew I was and if I needed a rest of course I should have one and meanwhile we'd just make this a brief, relaxed sort of expedition.

In the wood it was warm and still. The sandy hollow between the roots of our big tree seemed still to retain some of the heat of the day and as soon as we settled down together to wait I felt waves of fatigue lapping over me. I told Cora to give me a prod if the badgers appeared and shamelessly fell into a deep sleep. In my dreams Cora and I wandered in broad daylight through Okefield right up to our own gate, where Mother was leaning and beaming and saying: "Come in and have tea." We were friends for all the world to see, and the world approved. Everyone smiled and waved . . .

Suddenly I jerked awake. Something wild was panting and straining and heaving into my face—with fangs, foul breath, a lolling tongue. I screamed. Cora was there. A voice yelled: "Found them!" Hundreds of feet crashed through the bracken. We were surrounded by hordes of wild beasts and wild men. We clutched each other frantically and shrank into the roots of the tree . . . but brutish hands seized us, wrenched us apart, swung us bodily from the ground. Torches blazed down. I pulled my anorak over my face as I was heaved into position over a giant shoulder. Far away a voice murmured: "Real babes in the wood, eh?" I couldn't make nightmare of the reality or reality of the nightmare. Half-dreaming, through miles and miles of darkness, I swayed to and fro on the giant shoulder to the rhythm of the giant steps. And then we stopped, and the gruff murmur of voices stopped, and there was a crisp, sharp rat-a-tat on someone's door and the door opened and I was carried into a house and put gently down on a sofa. I sensed that all stood back. Still dreaming, I slowly uncovered my face and blinked up at the faces round about. Then Mother, ashen and distorted, dropped to her knees beside me, sank her face into my shoulder and sobbed as if her heart would break. Her hair, loosened for night, fell across my face. Her tears ran down on to my neck. I couldn't see. I didn't move.

❧ *Postscript* ❧

THAT WAS THE END OF EVERYTHING, OF COURSE. NOTHING about Okefield was ever quite the same. Eventually nice things happened again and it was a good place to be brought up in—Jo and Dory and I have always agreed about that. But that first year that I spent there, at Okington School, was completely separate from all the other years I lived there— and from all the years I'd lived in Birmingham too, come to that. I have no difficulty recalling the faces and events of that year, where other faces and events blur and merge too easily. I have only by chance to come across one of my few mementoes—the hobgoblin bracelet from Mrs. Briggs, a poem of Hermione's, Cora's mother's forget-me-not—and all the attendant details crowd back . . .

What had happened that night, of course, was quite predictable. My mother, concerned about my exhaustion, had gone to my room to check that all was well with me before settling down for her own night's sleep. She and Father had panicked when they realized I was missing from the house and had instantly remembered the strange winter visitations we'd had and some of Mrs. Phillips's more horrifying tales of thugs and vagrants on the common. They'd called in the police, a search had been organized, half the village had been roused, Mrs. Briggs had reported seeing children on the common in the vicinity of the wood on an earlier occasion . . . No effort had been spared. Policemen, torches, dogs, volunteer neighbours, Father, Mrs. Briggs, all, it seemed, had pounded up through the village, past the church, on to the common. With flails and staves they'd beaten back gorse and bracken in search of me. Little credence had been given to Mrs. Briggs's tale at this point, so nobody realized that Cora was missing too. I, alone, was believed kidnapped, murdered. Desperate urgency, terrible fear, was in every-body's heart. All for me. And then I was found with Cora —in the arms of the "Devil Child" . . .

I didn't return to school that term. It was near enough the summer holidays anyway. Mother and Father were never able to speak to me much about the entire episode; the topic became taboo in our household and Mother even had to get rid of Mrs. Briggs because she couldn't refrain from raising it. That was the only good result of the business. Hermione never spoke to me again; she went off to boarding-school after the holidays and our ways would have been bound to diverge from then on in any case. Susan never spoke to me again; she stayed on at Okington School, but my parents decided to move me to the state secondary school in Heatherton so, apart from passing her in the village now and again, I didn't see much of her either. Bar-bara started at Heatherton School with me and spoke to me once. She told me that her parents had forbidden her to have anything to do with me. I was to be an outcast as Cora had been. The only nice thing I've got to say about

Barbara is that she didn't spread black gossip about me among our new schoolmates in Heatherton and so, after a dismally lonely summer, I was able to make new friends quickly when school resumed. As it happened, Georgia Jamieson went on to Heatherton too and, in the end, we became firm friends.

I never saw Cora again. She and her father moved from the area within a day or two of our last fatal expedition and nobody ever knew where they'd gone. It became a village joke for people to flap their arms and say: "The Ravenwings have flown!" Everyone was delighted.

But I have always grieved for that lost friendship and wondered what became of Cora. That's why I've now written this account of our year together and mean to send it out for all to see. I am calling it simply *Cora Ravenwing* because I'd like Cora to read it and know what I thought— and who could resist buying a book with one's own name as the title?

Furthermore, I suspect that Cora is still living somewhere near Okefield. My parents, retired now, still live in the old family house and I visit them several times a year. Then I tramp again round my favourite haunts of long ago, the village streets, the common, the graveyard. There, one grave remains faithfully tended while the rest are now wild and overgrown. Round the back of the church, near the bell-tower, the roses on the grave of Myra Ravenwing still blossom and flourish as sweetly as they did all those years ago. Someone still returns frequently, someone for whom that spot is the most precious on earth. One of these days I shall crunch my way along the path beside the church, turn the corner, and there she'll be.